# THE REVERSE TAKEOVER — PART 1

## From Sweat Equity to Private Equity

Mary Duffy and Marc De Lima

We dedicate this novel to all the veterans who served their nation, but in particular to the fallen and returnees of the Vietnam War, their children, their families, and friends. The gothic and hallucinating experience that was Vietnam did not blunt our animal spirits of entrepreneurship, the force that impels the ideals and greatness of our country.

**Mary and Marc**

# Prologue: Watch Your Back!

Doctor Ivon Bates enjoyed a calm, carefree life in academia, having it all: youth, great wealth, brains, looks, health, and prestige. But the chilling news now on hold for him would change all that.

He thought he heard someone calling his name, but he simply shrugged. Earlier this morning he'd heard Cass mumble in her sleep: "You will lose laurel, trunk, and the plant, and the offshoots: an evil seed and a good seed."

In his cubicle, while busy at the two-horned microscope, Ivon Bates, Ph.D., Post-doctoral Associate, researcher, and assistant professor, was also trying to decipher Cassandra's words. But unable to make any sense out of the riddle, he opened the journal on T-cells and began reading it. Only after Bill Crabtree, the dyspeptic Senior Associate in charge, raised his voice did Dr. Bates look up.

"Bates, telephone!" said Crabtree, waving the receiver. "Are you deaf?"

With a vague sense of dread, Dr. Bates stepped up to Crabtree's desk, thinking that perhaps it was the payroll department: no time sheet, no pay. The Massachusetts Institute of Technology is a noble institution, but still a nasty bureaucracy. Crabtree handed him the receiver.

"Hello…Yes, this is he…Dead?"

His face as white as his lab coat, Dr. Bates looked at Crabtree. "Detective Wilkins? Midtown Precinct North on West 51st…I'll be all right…give me a minute." Clearing his throat, he tried to speak, but his throat felt parched. "Yes, of course," he said. "Tonight, for sure…Let me write it down."

Bill Crabtree pushed a yellow pad and a pen in front of Dr. Bates, who scrawled a few lines in uneven hand. "Yes, Midtown North on 51st." Putting the receiver down, he shuffled back to his cubicle, as Crabtree tore off the top sheet, trailing right behind him. "Bad news, Ivon?" he asked. But since Dr. Bates only stared at him, he handed him the sheet and asked again,

"Who's dead, Ivon?"

"My father's dead…murdered."

Stunned by the news, the other five associates huddled by Dr. Bates' cubicle, speaking in hushed tones, as a dim silence shrouded the lab, the blades of the two ceiling fans strumming, humming, and slicing the stillness of the day. So loudly did the telephone ring out once again that they all jumped, Crabtree cursing and rushing to answer. "Ivon, a Mr. Phil Kerdes," Crabtree said with a gentle tone, "the Controller at Bates Pharmaceuticals."

After exchanging a few words with Phil Kerdes, Dr. Bates dropped the receiver and with a faint voice he told Bill Crabtree, "If I get any more calls, please tell them I'll be there tonight. Now, I've got to pack and drive to Manhattan right away."

As he drove his Audi across the Charles River, he debated in his mind: Cassandra's going to be upset when I tell her I'm taking off for New York. A sweet woman, but also a royal pain. He parked the Audi and strode to his house with the ungainly gait of a tall man, his shoulders sagging. The old man worked all his life—with the frenzy of a mad workaholic—and what did he get?

In the thick July heat, he felt his T-shirt stick to his long torso. He saw the group of children playing quietly out front and three young mothers talking on the steps of the neighboring house. Isn't it odd…why are the kids noiseless today? Going through the side door, he passed the kitchen and plodded to the main bedroom. He overheard a giggle. Ah, Cassandra is on the telephone. How to break the news and not frighten her…what to say? Hesitating for a second, he stood frozen by the bedroom door, and since it was ajar, he heard her voice and loud laughter. Oh, Cass, Cassie, you're here to help me cope with this odd feeling that is neither pain nor grief.

Who's she talking to?

A stab of doubt pierced his heart, pulse throbbing as he stood and listened.

"Can't figure him out. Imagine a Yalie and MIT grad with a doctorate degree making thirty grand a year! He refuses to work for his father; he has no interest in business. But I want a firm commitment from you."

You. Who's you?

"Well…says his prayers, reads his Bible every night, goes to church on Sun- days…"

Feeling a hot shame blazing in his face, Dr. Bates padded out of there only to sit in his Audi, numb, his heart aching. To eavesdrop in other people's affairs can cause much unwanted pain. Oh, Cassandra, how could you? His father was dead and now this betrayal. Leaning his head on the headrest, he closed his eyes, as if wishing away the dismal feelings now clawing at his heart. But that didn't help, for he kept replaying Detective Wilkins' voice in his mind: Blunt instrument, maybe a lug wrench…two deep indentations…instant death. When he opened his eyes, he felt the blood in his veins throbbing and filling him with shame. With little warning, his stomach convulsed, barely giving him time to open the door, as he retched both through nose and mouth, his face breaking in a cold sweat.

After wiping his face clean with a handful of tissues, a strange melancholy set in his heart, and soon the thick air lulled him to shallow sleep. Suddenly, he felt presences shoving and shaking him and yanking his hair, the apparitions grunting, shrieking, and speaking to him in an ancient dialect. Horrified, he grasped their meaning: Much pain awaits you as surely as day follows our beloved mother Night, and you shall pay for the wicked crime you will commit. Terrified now, he saw another shape quietly sitting in the backseat. "You will pay for the sins of your father and that soulless Sabino. Until then," roared the fiend, "get on with your easy life. You will hear from me: Donato—also known as Legion, for we are many." The hoods and the unnatural shadows that engulfed them prevented Doctor Bates from seeing their faces, and as he focused harder, they faded as if they had passed through the glass and metal of the side doors.

Startled by the sound of a horn, he thought, What wicked crime…what sins…Three old homeless women and a monk! Never had he ever experienced such an intense dream, nor had he ever felt the nearness of fiends. To his dismay, he felt he had not seen the last of them. Not until he had composed himself did he march back to the house to face Cassandra.

"I've got to go to Manhattan tonight. My father is dead…murdered." Cassandra paled and rushed to his side. "I'll be away for a week."

"Oh, Ivon! Of course, go my dear darling, sweet angel, Ivon. I love you so much. Look at you, your eyes are red and your face blotchy!"

As he faced Cassandra, ready for a confrontation, he found he lacked the language of violence, and though he felt unfit—woefully unfit—he murmured,

"I am twenty-five years old; but I promise that buried behind me remains innocence."

When he ran his fingers through his hair, much to his astonishment, he winced at the pain he felt in his scalp. To make it worse, a bolt of terror made the hair on his neck and head stand erect as Phil Kerdes' warning echoed in his mind: They will try to kill you, too! He was sure Phil had called it…buyout. A hostile takeover. And that either Alex Panagora or Helen McCain—a wicked pair—may be behind father's murder.

"These two criminals are trying to steal the company—your company now, Ivon!" Phil Kerdes, the controller, had said.

Oh no! Bates Pharmaceuticals is father's company, Ivon thought. Dad and Sabino built it from nothing; two men of valor, two prisoners of war who made their escape not by lamenting but by acting, not with words but with deeds. Two Vietnam War heroes who as soldiers earned Silver Stars, Bronze Stars, and Purple Hearts, while as civilians built a thriving manufacturing company. Only after he was ready to leave did he see clearly through Cassandra's grimace of grief. She is wearing a mask; he thought. Never in his life had he felt so bitter. He searched for a trace of sympathy on her face in vain. Saying nothing or even taking a second look at her, he stepped out the door.

With a clear head—and the objectivity of the scientist he was—he assessed what he was up against: a murder to solve, a duplicitous girlfriend, a death threat over his head, and an industrial company to run and keep afloat. Once outside, he made the solemn vow to unmask his father's killer, not because of duty or filial love, but because he now felt he was next on the killer's list. They will try to kill you too! Neither vengeance, nor love—God knows his entire life had been a loveless life; a life in which he had felt unwanted, and if not reviled, at least ignored by his father—or duty motivated him.

Survival did.

That such disgraces could occur, he did not want to believe. Still, less did he believe they could happen to him, but they did, and now he had to go outside the safe walls of academia and face the accidental world.

# Chapter 1 — The Bates Pharmaceuticals Plant

When the limo came to a full stop by the front iron gates, young Doctor Ivon Bates, without waiting for his driver to come around to open the door, grabbed his briefcase and stepped out into the cold and windy November morning. Raising his eyes, he read the Plant's enormous sign: BATES PHARMACEUTICALS; the huge, slanted white letters straining to leap out of the red-orange background. That is a strange sign, he thought, father's sign since he always thought big.

By the wide-open gates, glancing over his left shoulder, he saw Tom—Tom B. Stone.

Stone, the Plant Manager, his dark face a shade paler than usual, talking to the division managers and supervisors, who listened with anxious looks in their eyes. To listen in, Ivon stood still by the closed door, his body leaning over, his ear cocked. Oh, no! No eavesdropping, he chided himself, stepping away. As he headed toward the research laboratories, Tom's garbled voice lingered in his ears. Union thugs…rabble-rousers…

Young Dr. Ivon Bates was tall, twenty-five years old, with a quick smile and clumsy gait. He was now running Bates Pharmaceuticals, the company he had inherited from his father, Joe Bates. The sharp smells of formaldehyde, iodine, and the exhaust from the Bunsen burners hit his nostrils. Glancing at his watch, he quickened his pace, his steps echoing along the bare walls. But as he reached the raised landing of the stairs that led to the labs, he heard loud screams: "Help! Help! Lenox is in trouble."

Firing a look toward the loading dock, Dr. Bates saw Felix and another worker, both dressed in light-blue work uniforms, kneeling, trying to revive a fallen worker. When he got there, Felix, a veteran Bates worker, looked up and said, "It's Lenox, Ivon! He was washing the ice from the platform with the hot water hose when he lost control and slipped. I saw him fall face down and bang his head against the floor."

Doctor Bates examined Lenox. "He's knocked out, but his pulse is strong." The young blond worker said, "Man, that hose was whipping and shooting hot scalding water all over the place. You need powerful hands to hold that high-pressure hose."

"This is Joey. Joey De Lemos," said Felix, adding, "his first week here and Tom asked me to show him around. After this week he'll help Dr. Loomis in Syrups." "Me and Joey just came from Customs with that shipment Tom's been expecting from Germany, when we saw Lenox washing the dock," Felix explained. "*Alla* sudden he slipped, and that damned hose went crazy coiling and snapping, throwing hot boiling water all over the place. Good thing Joey turned it off, or Lenox would have been a mess." He paused, and gazing at Joey with teary eyes, he exclaimed, "Joey saved his life! I couldn't move fast enough myself on account of my bad leg, but Joey *heah* did and saved him."

Dr. Bates stared at the young blond worker's head and the strange way in which the young man wore his striking yellow hair. Perhaps bleached, Doctor Bates surmised. A gleam in the kid's eyes stirred in Dr. Bates a wisp of a memory that he couldn't place. Those green eyes are so striking in that tanned face; what a strange feeling! Removing his topcoat, Dr. Bates placed it on the wet wooden floor. "Here, Joey," he said, "Give me a hand, let's roll him off the wet floor onto the coat—gentle, very gentle." Lenox, face up, began groaning, his eyelids fluttering, as if he was trying to come to. For an instant his eyelids opened and the white of his eyes rolled up, the groaning turning into gentle snoring.

"Oh, man," said Joey, "I was afraid he was gonna wake up." Again, Lenox groaned and his eyelids fluttered.

With alarm in their eyes, Dr. Bates and the blond kid looked at each other. The young blond man shook his head and said, "I hope the ambulance gets here soon, man. If Lenox comes to and starts feeling the burn pain…mama mia! It's going to be tough for Lenox; the pain may throw him into shock. Bummer, man. Even when I have a small little burn on my finger or something, I'm hurting the whole day."

In a few minutes, Tom B. Stone—the big boss at the Plant—arrived. And close at his heels was Janos Panko, the division manager of Vitamins, Pills, and Capsules. "A rescue helicopter is on its way, Ivon," Tom Stone said, out of breath, as he kneeled to check the unconscious man. "I had to cash in a few favors, but they're sending a rescue team—a helicopter!" When Tom and Janos undressed Lenox, they shook their heads and gasped in horror. Dr. Bates felt both a rush of pity rise to his heart, and a heavy dull pain sink in the pit of his stomach, lodging there with a thud. Ghastly blisters! The poor man will be in pain for a long time.

"Holy mother of God!" exclaimed Janos Panko, who was a thick, beefy man with blond, brush-bristle, hair, a bully, and a racist who terrorized his workers. The group of onlookers strained their necks to get a closer view. Although Dr. Bates wasn't a medical doctor, he saw that Lenox had suffered third-degree burns on his upper torso and on part of his legs where the skin had buckled up. Patches of huge blisters glistened in the wintry daylight. After a closer view, some workers shook their heads in quiet horror and squirmed, but others seemed spell-bound and calm. Three women in uniform started weeping and consoling one another. Then Dr. Bates heard Pia, the chief Cost Accountant, pray in a pious trembling voice:

"There shall be a fall that befalls thee, and a plague that plagues thy dwelling."

Dr. Bates thought, Pia is such a goofball, but she means well, but why is she always sermonizing? And why does she wear those frumpy dresses? She tugged at the elastic band of her undergarments and snapped it loudly. Fixing her eyes to the ceiling and stretching both arms high up, she exclaimed,

"I sought the Power, and He heard me, and delivered me from all my fears."

"Hush, Pia," said Tom Stone. "Ask Melissa to bring some accident report forms." Pia Pecunia nodded and trotted off.

The young blond man pricked up his ears: "The chopper's here!"

Within thirty seconds, the rescue helicopter became visible in front of the loading dock, hovering, swirling down gently in the parking lot. Dr. Bates watched the three white-frocked men jump out, slide off a foldable gurney and rush in, while the pilot kept the engine running, waiting inside the glass bubble of the helicopter, its tinted glass reflecting the feeble wintry sunshine. Tom must have put some pressure on the hospital, Dr. Bates thought. They wasted no time. The senior paramedic brought his walkie-talkie close to his lips.

"Hawkeye to Yeager: we're coming out," the voice crackling with sharp static.

The helicopter lifted and soared over the employee parking

lot. Loud, snappy orders made Dr. Bates turn around.

"All right, all right, people!" yelled Janos Panko. "Go back to work—you don't get paid to gawk around the hallways. Let's go, let's go, move it!" Most of the workers moved on, as Janos stood with his hands on his waist, scowling. Since a small group lingered, ignoring him, he clapped his hands and bellowed,

"Move it! Let's go people. Let's go! What the hell are you hanging around for?"

No sooner had he said this when a voice taunted him, "Hang your mother, Janos." Turning beet-red and scratching his groin, Janos craned his neck, attempting to recognize the wise guy.

Surprised, and a trifle annoyed by Janos' rough manner, Dr. Bates stared at him and though he wanted to say something—if not scold him or challenge him, at least admonish him—he kept quiet, his eyes narrowing as if deciding what, or what not to do. Were it not for Tom Stone, who had been watching him, an altercation would have ensued. To defuse the awkward situation, Tom asked Dr. Bates to follow him to the edge of the loading dock, where they examined the tip of the hose and the layers of ice on the wooden platform. In the daylight, Dr. Bates noted that Tom Stone's lips and bulbous nose were twitching. Of course, Tom's angry—or upset to be more accurate—and who wouldn't be, since all the problems ended up on his lap.

Tom said, "A good man, Lenox—had a rough time when his wife left him; he had to raise his son, Lenox Jr., all by himself. Young Lenox must be about your age, Ivon, maybe a few years younger."

Dr. Bates saw a red GM Sierra pickup with stenciled, slanted lettering on the door—Bates Pharmaceuticals, Inc.—pull up by the side door. The driver, with great agility, stepped up on the six-step yellow-painted metal staircase and went through the side door. "Sabino's here," said Dr. Bates, admiring the spring and energy in the old man's legs.

He shook hands with the old man.

"I saw the helicopter. What happened, Tom?" asked the old man, looking at Tom Stone, who recounted the incident in a few words. The old man kicked the hose,

"This pisses me off! I told Lenox to have another man turn the pressure on and off and to wear the logger mitts. Next time somebody disobeys my orders, there's going to be hell to pay."

The group of workers who had been lingering around the platform disbanded. A tall African American woman stepped up to Dr. Bates and said, "I'll get your coat cleaned Dr. Bates, and I'll give it to Victor." Dr. Bates exchanged glances with Tom Stone, but neither said anything not wanting to upset Sabino any further; but also because both were afraid of him. After an awkward moment of dead silence, Dr. Bates changed the subject.

"Felix says he just picked up the German shipment."

"It's about time!" said Sabino.

Sabino was a laconic, strange, and aloof man. Only after Sabino calmed down did Dr. Bates put his right hand on Sabino's shoulder in a warm gesture. As he got close to him, he saw the deep furrows in the old man's brow, the countless fine lines etched in his weathered face, and all that thick, snow-white hair. Yes, a strange man indeed: one fiery eye and the other one made dull by the heavy droop of the eyelid and a furry eyebrow that hid a ridged scar. Sabino was now the sole survivor of the ten original founders who had accompanied Joe Bates — crossing the Hudson River, and riding on the George Washington Bridge—on that fated July 6th, 1970. Strange the way things happen, Joe Bates being killed on July 6th, too.

What a man, Sabino—Engineer and Deputy Plant Man—nothing ever escapes his attention, and even that nasty Janos Panko, a powerful man and twice Sabino's size, fears him. Doctor Bates felt that without Sabino, his father could never have built the company to the size it is now. He was father's hit man. Young Dr. Bates had known Sabino all his life. A warm feeling washed down Dr. Bates' chest as the image of him as a toddler tagging at the heels of Sabino flashed in his mind. He saw the mysterious, tiny, iridescent rock—a tiny sphere—Sabino had found in the swamp. It's so bright, Sabino, it hurts my eyes! Hearing next Sabino's words, promising that one day that little rock would unlock the mystery of the universe; if he was a good boy and grew up to be a man of right.

Little Ivon would always ask, "What is a man of right, Sabino?" And Sabino's perennial, playful answer was,

"An upright man!"

Only when Ivon was about fifteen years old did Sabino give

him a more direct answer: "An upright man is a man that fears God, defends his women, and honors them with nobility—God and honor, Ivon; or what is man for?"

Looking west, from where they were standing, Dr. Bates saw the winding dirt road and the bend where the swamp and the marshes started. As Sabino turned sideways, Dr. Bates observed the incipient carcinomas on Sabino's neck: a tough, leathery, thick neck with deep creases burned by the sun and the wind from the marshes. And at a right angle to Sabino's left earlobe, Dr. Bates could also see a second scar, a lustrous scar that seemed filled with ashes, that people said he got when he was a prisoner of war in Vietnam.

The Latino workers would say it was *la cachetada del diablo*—the devil's slap—and as they said that, they would make the sign of the cross two or three times.

Tom Stone informed Dr. Bates that he was upset because he'd heard rumors that some outsiders were agitating the workers to have a vote for a local Union. Dr. Bates put his hand on Tom's shoulder. "Let's wait on this," he said. As Dr. Bates moved on, he added, "I'll be working with Dr. Norris this morning, and I'm so excited that Annie's bringing her experiments to a fruitful conclusion." Dr. Bates' cell phone rang, and he talked briefly with Phil O. Kerdes, Bates Pharmaceuticals' Controller. "That was Phil reminding me he has a crucial luncheon meeting with our bankers about renewing a loan."

Sabino's droopy eyelid twitched. "Old Phil is not like your father, Ivon. Phil's not to be trusted," he said. "You'll have to step in to kick some ass with them bankers yourself. Don't leave it up to Phil. I will never trust that paper-pusher, number-cruncher—pea-counter!"

"You think this Union business has anything to do with father's murder?" "I doubt it," said Tom Stone. "What do you think, Sabino?"

"No way! I'll deal with these Union thugs in due time. Phil made it clear to me that Helen McCain's henchman, her chief of security—a man named Rashkin—killed Joe. That woman's evil and she might want to come after you or send a paid assassin. Keep an eye on Phil and also on Alex Panagora, that pompous ass Aussie, Greek, or whatever the hell he is—both rub me the wrong way."

Tom Stone asked, "Anything new with the cops, Ivon?"

“Detective Wilkins is on the case full-time; in fact, I’m meeting with him next week.” As Dr. Bates headed toward the labs, he smiled with anticipation, for he was eager to learn about Annie’s—Dr. Ana G. Norris, Director of Research — progress with the research. But Sabino’s warning popped into his mind and fear crept into his heart.

A paid assassin!

He felt his mouth dry, and he thought for an instant that his heart was failing, as he felt the sphincter in his esophagus strangle with violent spasms. For a fraction of a second, he felt the urge to flee out of the Plant, hearing himself direct Victor, his loyal driver, to rush him back to his apartment in Manhattan. Ah, yes! There, in his safe place, he would don his tunic and make himself invisible and impervious to threats.

Even as he composed himself, Phil Kerdes’ warning resonated in his mind: They will try to kill you, too. Only when he thought of Dr. Norris—her sweet smile, her astounding insights found in no other women—did he calm down, enjoying the anticipation of the nearness of her body. “Time to see sweet Annie,” he whispered between his teeth.

But a horrible thought spoiled his fun: What if she’s part of the conspiracy that killed father. She knows all the formulas and secrets — she could be a greedy woman wearing a mask!

# Chapter 2 — The Orbis People

With energetic steps, Helen McCain, the Chief Executive Officer of Orbis Laboratories, hurried along the hallway, happy that she was on the right course to meet all her goals, that this new man, Lowmax, was going to be a team player.

Halting for one second, she pondered: With old Joe Bates out of the picture, Bates Pharmaceuticals is up for grabs. I will buy them out! Heh heh heh. Yet she knew it wasn't going to be a simple task. No siree! She understood Sabino was a dangerous man—with that droopy eyelid always twitching and signaling he could slit your throat any time—not a man to toy with. Absolutely not.

As she trotted to the head of the table, the room fell silent. McCain scanned around. "Gentlemen, I'm running on a tight schedule today. But I want to see Lester's new gadgets this morning, so I'll be brief," she said, sighing as if resigned to have to meet with them. Aren't they a sorry bunch of boobs? McCain was a tall woman, with a strange deformity in her spine that pulled her shoulders back and made her bosom stick out like a half-moon. She wore prosthetic brassieres because in her thirties she had lost her right breast to cancer.

"These marketing stats suck," McCain continued, now glowering at Jerry Kagan, the Marketing V.P., whom her niece had married much against her wishes. "It's tough competing with Bates' prices," said Jerry Kagan. "Bates also has this guy Alex Panagora who's a ruthless salesperson, a high-power marketer, someone I'd love to have on our team."

"All I hear is excuses. Let me finish here with Henry and Lester," McCain said with an abrupt hand swipe, and gazing at Delmar Gotti and Jerry Kagan, she dismissed them. When Gotti and Kagan went out the door, the atmosphere relaxed. Camilla, McCain's executive secretary, walked in and announced, "Dr. Webber called. He said it was urgent. Also, the three Samurais want to see you." Camilla was a fine-figured woman in her mid-forties, dressed in a gray-striped tailored suit.

McCain cleared her throat. "Tell Doctor Webber I'll call him after I'm done here, and tell the Samurais I will see them, but for only five minutes. Give me half an hour." Turning her attention to Henry Cook, she thought, oh, 'dapper' Henry, must you always look dashing? What woman doesn't go for a barrel-chested and thick-armed man? McCain respected Henry Cook—her executive V.P.—for his skills with the technical side of running a medium-sized corporation, but derided him for lacking vision. Ah, yes, she mused, those stock options I set aside for you are locking you in, huh? Heh, heh, heh. Early in the year, Helen McCain had bought out Orbis Laboratories, Inc., for herself and some of her friends on the Board of Directors and had assigned enough stock options to put Henry in the million-dollar circle.

With a sour look on her face, she said, "I hear the Bates people are going ape-shit over a new drug. And if Bates is going to market a new product that will cause our own sales to go down, I want to know."

"I'll pump Alex Panagora, their marketing director," said Henry Cook.

"You heard Jerry's excuses. He has tons of people with MBAs in marketing, all kinds of detail-reps and they can't move our products. Suckers couldn't even sell a dime for a nickel to save their lives."

Staring at both Cook and Lester Lowmax, she said in a soft tone, "I'm counting on you—both of you—to save this company. Orbis Labs depends on you now. Together, we'll make Orbis a world leader, but I can't do it alone. I need you both by my side—as a team we can't fail!" Next, she addressed Lester,

"The cat got your tongue, Lester?"

Lowmax looked at her, confused.

Her eyes bored on Orbis' Director of Security with an unspoken but certain message: "Hit the gym Lester, do something about that gut hanging over your belt!" McCain hired Lowmax one month after the Secret Service canned him for financial crimes and money laundering, to fill the vacancy left by Orbis' former Director Peter Rashkin, who had disappeared without a trace. What if they let him go? Yeh, yeah, Lowmax made a mistake and seduced an underage girl, and extorted money from some wealthy creatures. It wasn't a big deal, and yet they kicked him out without a pension! To maneuver with ease and with excellent results, a man with balls needs room and here he is…plenty of room here at Orbis Laboratories, to be sure. McCain stood up and the other two did too, stepping out to the accounting area. Henry Cook cleared his throat and said, "Alex Panagora, the marketing guy Jerry mentioned, is unhappy at Bates Pharmaceuticals and is looking around."

"Let me lean on the Bates people," added Lowmax. "Slow them down."

"You'll have your chance to be lean and mean. May I suggest something, Lester?"

"Of course, Helen."

"Put a tail on Ivon Bates. I want to know every move he makes, who he talks to, where he goes, what he does day and night, even what he eats for breakfast. Build a dossier. If we put the fear of God in him, he'll turn tail and sell. I know human nature and let me tell you that this young man has neither the guts nor the street-smarts that his old man had."

"I'll do some of the shadowing myself and will keep you posted."

"Wonderful! Excellent attitude, Lester. Some tasks you can't delegate. Now, you could spook him enough to see how he takes it…soften him up before we blow him away." Grinning, McCain bared her horsy, yellow teeth.

"Did you warn Lester about Sabino?" Henry Cook asked McCain.

"Yes, he knows all about Sabino—Sabino, the Body Snatcher. Joe Bates would not have been able to build Bates Pharmaceuticals without Sabino watching his back. He's the only damned foreigner and immigrant I will ever respect. Some tough hombre this Sabino is; a tough mutt—half Peruvian, half Japanese. Only in the USA will you find these tough half-breeds."

Turning to Henry Cook, she whispered in his ear, "I want you and Delmar and his senior accounting people to get moving with those offshore limited partnerships. They are great tax havens, and I don't see why we couldn't open a hundred instead of the few we own. And it's all legal!" McCain changed the subject: "Let's go down to the Security office, Lester, and you can show me that Control Room you've been bragging about."

"We call it the Panopticon," corrected Lester Lowmax with a pedantic tone, "which is a term much richer than 'Control Room.' In fact, it comes from a difficult philosophical book I've been reading; it means permanent watching, security—analogous to Las

Vegas-style vigilance."

Analogous? Vigilance? Sneering, McCain muttered under her breath, "Who gives a snapping turtle's ass what you call it! Pompous ass! Panopticon? Why not call it Exhorbiton? God knows Big Brother didn't come cheap."

Exasperated, she snapped, "Well, show me the damn machine, or did it go to take a leak?"

A few minutes later, chief Lowmax showed Henry Cook and Helen McCain the power of his new pride and joy, his hi-tech baby. McCain muttered to herself, you may call it your baby, but it's my money—you jackass! To Lowmax: "Is the system wired to the mainframe, the LANs, the WANs, and the new digitized telephone system?"

"Yes, of course, it's one hundred percent integrated, and Y2K sound. In five years, the year 2000 will rain disaster on all computers and we must be ready for that."

Very impressive, Lester the Molester!

Sitting down at the main console, Lowmax flipped switches, typed commands, and pushed the speaker button. As the speakers squawked, Lowmax smiled a triumphant, crooked smile that hid his crooked teeth. "That's Michelle Depardieu in Accounts Payable." He typed a few commands on the keyboard and the screen split in three windows: one contained the data Michelle was entering, the second Michelle's ID picture and personal data, and the third, a layout of the Payables area.

Helen McCain exclaimed, "terrific graphics!"

Picking up the thread again, Lowmax said, "The next step is to plug in the video satellite communications systems: ACTS—Advanced Communication Technology Satellite."

How impressive, Lester the Molester!

Cursing below her breath, McCain felt that the technology was leaving her behind. What's all this Newspeak? It's an Orwellian nightmare: woofs, whistles, bits, bytes, gates, and buffers. Programs follow protocols. They expunge and are expunged, reside, migrate, and they even catch viruses. Next, they'll be fornicating! Damn all that gibberish about mouse drops, digital soup, bugs! And get a load of Lester Lowmax; he's as smug as a bug in a rug.

Henry Cook asked, "You remember that hacker who wanted thirty grand to set up a firewall? He'll do it for ten grand but wants to use the system whenever he is in the City. I hope you give me permission. We'll pick his brain and he'll pick a few digital locks for us."

McCain's scowl faded. "Henry, you're always one step ahead of me. I love that." Next, she made a mental note to ask Henry, in private, which digital locks he had in mind. The Justice Department? The Food and Drug Administration? The SEC? Would luv to see why the FDA is dragging its feet with our products.

Lester Lowmax continued, "We need someone to ram through backdoors and Trojans."

Confused, McCain stared at Lester.

Damn you Lester the Molester!

What's he talking about? Backdoors and Trojans? That sounds so obscene. She felt that Henry and Lester made an odd couple, and mused: Ah, Henry 'the Eight' Cook—famed for a personal endowment measured in inches—and Lester the Molester: predator and salt and assault of sultry pubescent Lolitas!

Smiling with irrepressible glee, McCain returned to her office. Soon we'll have instant link with Seoul, Singapore, Taiwan, Beijing, and Tokyo. Orbis Laboratories will now sell more of that stuff to the North Koreans. No more snooping by the Feds, the SEC, the FDA, the Drug Enforcement Agency, the New York District Attorney, and the dumb cops. She pranced around her desk, essaying a few old-fashioned Twist steps, her heavy bosom jiggling sideways.

McCain was paranoid of both industrial espionage and Government snooping, but now Henry the Eight's grasp of technology with Chief Lowmax's street-smart skills had given her renewed faith for the future. Neither Government spies nor competitors will stop us!

Camilla's uneasy voice squawked on the intercom, "Dr. Webber's on the line again, Helen. Says it's urgent—he's got bad news!"

Bad news? What the hell is the Kraut's problem? Let's handle it right now:

"Put his Nazi-ass through."

But she cooled her fiery temper, knowing that Doctor Webber—the Nazi—had come up with some excellent products in the past. That antianxiety drug was a mega seller and what about that potassium supplement for breast cancer? Ah, incredible sellers! But some of his ideas had been laughable, too. Once he had asked the executive committee for millions of dollars to research a drug for male senior citizens—to cure erectile dysfunction.

Sally Strong, the vice-chairman, had rebuffed him and shut him up with a series of pointed questions: "Aren't we displaying a male chauvinist attitude, Dr. Webber? Why not a drug for women? Don't women have a libido, too? And how do you market such a drug in a country where words such as penis, vagina, and breasts are taboo on radio, television, and in print?"

McCain pushed the speaker button. "I'm glad you called, Dr. Webber," she said with a saccharine voice. "What's up?"

"Helen, I'm afraid we'll have to junk Novatol-6. The staff and I will recommend that we suspend human clinical trials."

"This is bad news. I'll ask Camilla to check my schedule. We need to meet with Fred Stoller, Sally Strong, and John Underhill—the Executive Committee." You goddamned kraut! "We need to talk about a strategy. The Market. The Press. You better come prepared because there'll be lots of questions. Let's meet in a week." Novatol-6 was a fast-acting calcium blocker that had offered lots of hope for sufferers of high-blood pressure, and now all that revenue has gone to pot!

Helen McCain paused. "Not a word of this to anyone."

Dr. Webber cleared his throat. "Not a word to anyone, I promise. I've been in touch with the subcontractor in North Carolina; they just reported the tenth case of horrible side effects."

"What effects?"

"Ghastly mouth ailments: rotting gums and crumbling teeth. One of them broke out with ulcers on the tongue. It's messy. We must clean up this mess somehow."

"Any fatalities?"

"Two."

"Fax me the names. I'll get our legal department to visit relatives and start probing for an amount that will keep the families mum." McCain remained silent for a long time. "I'm going to Wichita Falls and Washington next Tuesday. It's about that Medicaid and Medicare. The Justice Department is claiming that we filed false tests results."

"See you in a week, Helen. And thanks for your continued support."

Support my ass, McCain thought. With her eyes narrowing and right eyelid twitching out of control, she pushed the 'End' button. She felt her heart thumping, a rage boiling inside her bosom and brains. Damn Kraut! This is a blow: all that research money wasted millions of dollars. What a terrible setback! Tipping back on her high back tufted chair, her white-blue mane in sharp contrast to the oxblood-hued leather of her chair, she forced herself not to scream. "Bad news clogs your arteries and makes you old," she mumbled. And in that instant, she felt older than her proper age.

On her fifty-seventh birthday, last August 31st, she had become Orbis' major shareholder in a swift leveraged buyout that made investors shake their heads in disbelief. What financial foul plays—you ninnies! The dust's settled by now. McCain saw the LBO as the major achievement of her career, but not her last. Certainly not! She rebuked herself. The compelling vision is to make Orbis an international powerhouse. Heh heh heh—I will, I will, I will. The essence of leadership is vision: Moses saw a vision and Saul a mission. Vast difference! Not that she concerned herself with African Americans, but she recognized that while Martin Luther King Jr. had a vision for his people, Jesse Jackson and Al Sharpton had a mission. Tom Brokaw, Dan Rather, and Larry King interviewed Helen McCain the week of the takeover and she became a celebrity. The following week, she made the front page of Newsweek, Businessweek, and Money. The New York Times and the Wall Street Journal also ran lengthy articles on the buyout. Woman of the year! No stopping that telephone from ringing. Camera crews, paparazzi, and autograph seekers couldn't get enough of her.

The footage for the successful TV program Biography1995 grew and editors kept busy developing a profile that they showed with the segments for General Colin Powell, Ross Perot, and Bill Gates. Of all the biographical facts the media had unearthed, she loathed the part about her mother having died in a mental institution, and never wanted to talk about it to anyone. Nor did she even want to think about it since she lived in constant fear of going insane herself.

Orbis Laboratories' destiny is to become not only a major

world-class company but also a dominant multinational. China to begin with...goals to carry out—not in slow years or by snail mail—at light speed. Neither competitors, nor foreigners, nor the Feds will get in the way of manifest destiny. How much is the slap on the wrist going to cost? Whatever the cost, Orbis will deny any legal liability, will plead *nolo contondere*—and pay.

Like sprinters to a finish line, several disjointed ideas that had been meandering in her mind rushed together as she sat there rubbing her temples, and in a flash she saw what she had to do.

Buy Bates Pharmaceuticals out—swamp and all! They have those wild acres of wetland out in New Jersey that developers could die for—to drain and build condos. By now, nobody remembers that ghosts and vampires used to live in that old gothic building. Sabino Yamamoto cleaned up that place, just as he cleaned up the old factory Joe had in Manhattan. Those were years of survival for old Joe. Ah! Joe Bates—a man with brass balls—he knew what he was doing when he risked buying that run-down factory.

That guy Alex Panagora must be a top marketer or he wouldn't be outselling Orbis. I have the vision, she murmured, and Lester Lowmax and—my soon-to-be-new acquisition—Alex Panagora will carry out the mission. When she brought her hand down, a diabolical delight shone in her dour face, and she sat for some time in somber splendor. Jerking herself to her feet, overcome with joy and unwilling to control herself, she flapped her arms against her sides and burst out in loud, wheezing laughter. Let's court, cajole, and pull Lester the Molester's strings—a puppet needs a puppeteer. The future is ours.

But her mind bore her back to the past. Poor Ivon Bates. She felt she should have taken care of him years ago, but she'd been confused and depressed. And it wasn't possible with that non-English speaking Antonia hanging around shooting dirty looks, mumbling her gibberish in Spanish. Oh! How he'd scream when I'd get near him. I wonder if Antonia or Cecilia ever mentioned to him he was always unwanted."

Camilla's husky voice came on the intercom: "Helen, it's the LIC plant again."

"Can this wait?"

"It's urgent. We had another break-in; please don't get upset, please. Joe Devlin is holding."

Only after a few seconds of intense self-control did she reply: "Put his ass through!"

# Chapter 3 — Rabbit City

When Dr. Bates pulled the metal door open, the pungent odor, shrieks, grunts, and thumps of the caged animals assaulted his nostrils and ears. Although the sign on the door read LAB VIVARIUM, and even though the lab also housed monkeys, rats, and mice, everyone in the Plant called it "Rabbit City."

"Wow, busy place!" Ivon thought.

A row of technicians bent at their double-headed microscopes nodded. As Dr. Bates ambled along the long stainless-steel counters toward Dr. Norris's office, he waved and smiled. Noting the outdated imaging equipment, he sighed. It's high time to order the new gamma cameras, the SPECT, and that other imaging equipment, he decided. Doctor Bates felt that Phil Kerdes mustn't dictate the equipment needed in the labs, since he knew little about scientific research. Phil may be a financial genius, but he is no expert in the lab equipment.

"How's Jack doing today, Annie?"

"He's in good shape, Ivon," answered Dr. Norris. The three women wearing light blue uniforms, who had been helping Dr. Norris with an image-guided biopsy, returned to their stations. Annie led Ivon into her office. "But we'll know better in two weeks; his vitals are fine and he looks great!" Dr. Norris wore a crisp white lab coat, and her black lustrous hair fell to her shoulders and sparkled under the bright overhead lamp.

"What's next?"

"This week we'll complete testing for clinical adverse effects. And next week, Jack will have some fun as we check for fertility. You know…sex…the great mating dance." Dr. Norris smiled, showing small white teeth and a twinkle in her eyes, as she looked up at Dr. Bates' face. Ivon felt mellow and warm around her, and the nearness of her body made the hair on his neck tingle.

"Fertility?"

"Oh, I had this idea that perhaps an enzyme could stir up an animal's libido. And if that is possible, we could do it with humans. The potential for such a drug is limitless!"

"Aren't we toying with nature here, Annie?"

"Well, yes, but positively: to heed the Lord's word—procreate."

Not to inhibit her, he nodded—to show his approval—and changed the subject. "Phil wants me to spend a few days at headquarters. Cash is tight, and he wants to go over the problem with me. Go as far as you can on your own with that cancer research."

"Any word from the police?"

"I'm meeting with Detective Wilkins next week. He's checking some leads and wants to bring me up to date; he's certain it wasn't a professional hit. And I'm happy he's making progress. He is optimistic, but what is important is that he hasn't given up."

"I read in the newspapers that Orbis' former chief of security has disappeared. Who knows, maybe that man—Rashkin—killed your father and fled the country." Seeing the hurt in Dr. Bates' eyes, she shifted her tone. "I hear Lenox had an accident—was he on drugs or drunk?"

"A freak accident, I guess," he replied, criticizing himself for not thinking of the cause of the accident. "His breath smelled of liquor. Later, I'm going to stop by the hospital to see Lenox on my way to Manhattan, so I won't be here for the rounds."

"I don't want to sound pushy, but soon we should talk about formalizing a contract for the results of the cancer research. You know your father agreed to my co-owning the patent, but we never got around to putting it in writing and I…"

Ivon froze for a second, for the idea of anyone co-owning a piece of Bates Pharmaceuticals was anathema to him—even a sin. Recovering and interrupting her, he exclaimed, "Fine, fine, let's talk about it next week. Meanwhile, I'll consult with Phil Kerdes and Tom. We'll see what they have to say."

"But Ivon, your father and I had an agreement, and it is now between us. Phil and Tom had nothing to do with it."

Adopting a deflecting tone, he said, "No problem, Annie. Let's discuss it next week—okay?" He gave a quick look around, as if to make sure no one was looking. Satisfied, he advanced to Annie's side and said playfully, "Look straight ahead." Annie—a trifle puzzled—obeyed. Ivon said, "You have the most beautiful profile I've ever seen in a woman." Annie held her green eyes downwards in utter surprise.

"See you soon, Annie," said Ivon and he walked away thinking, She has no basis, no right or otherwise, to make such a claim. Imagine Scrooge Joe Bates agreeing to co-own a patent! The poor dear is delirious.

Annie was a gorgeous woman. But according to him, a delirious, gorgeous woman, who had to be dealt with. With patience and the right touch, he felt, the alley cat would soon be in the bag—the sack! Let them know you think they are special; make them feel special even though they are not and then get rid of them before they get rid of you.

As he was leaving, he saw Felix and Joey De Lemos pushing a hand truck loaded with boxes and metal containers. He held the doors open for them.

Felix said, "Miss Meneses says we have to store this shipment on this floor, because she's running out of room downstairs."

"Yo, bro!" exclaimed Joey, wrinkling his nose and looking at Dr. Bates. "This place stinks like a bus-stop bathroom, man. Worse than an outhouse, a whore-house, and the White House put together. Phewwww! Animal House. Stinko-rama mama."

Joey De Lemos was slender, two or three notches below six feet. He wore a gold ring in one ear. His hair showed a three-step cut: below his ears and around half of the lower head the hair was thick and brown, the stubble growing in, and a blond rat-tail stuck out on his neck. The top of the head exploded in a shock of striking gold blond gathered in a short ponytail.

Looking at the kid and smiling, Dr. Bates felt clueless about what to say or how to react to the kid's sassy speech. What's this 'bro' business? And that haircut! At least it's not a Mohawk. But he's a good-looking kid despite that hideous haircut. There's more to Joey De Lemos than the mask he wears. Then he heard the distinct sound of a gunshot. Panic seized him for a fraction of a second as he imagined that a paid murderer was shooting his way in and coming to the third floor to find him and kill him.

Only after Felix and Joey were out the door did he react, and with cautious steps, followed them.

***

When Victor, Dr. Bates' limo driver, saw that a masked man was smashing the headlights of the vans, he had run toward the man shouting, "Hey, hey, what the hell are you doing!" The startled thug had drawn a gun and with a trembling hand had pulled—by accident—the trigger, missing Victor by a yard. Hitting the ground and rolling behind a shipping container, Victor had vaulted through the gates screaming, "There is a crazy guy with a gun! Tom…get Sabino…somebody get Sabino!"

After smashing the parking lights, the windshields, and the rear windows of the three delivery vans parked by the loading dock, the masked man sprinted toward the parked Honda. But gusts of freezing wind lashing out of the swamp impeded the man's escape.

Within a minute, Sabino Yamamoto appeared at the side door of the loading dock, holding a shotgun in his right hand. The thug saw him and hurried to the waiting Honda, which took off with a loud squeal, screeching and lurching forward, the engine revving up. Seconds later, Felix, Joey, and Dr. Bates poured out from the same side door. Dr. Bates saw Sabino advance, holding a gun with his right hand, a gun that seemed weightless in his large, gnarled hand. It was a stainless steel, short-barreled, 12-gauge, pump-action shotgun. He aimed it and blasted the Honda's rear window. At the crack of the shot, a flock of marsh ducks and bands of sparrows and meadowlarks rose over the marshes, shrieking and squalling. Dr. Bates watched them disappear west beyond the marsh.

The Honda lurched forward. Sabino kept walking behind the fleeing Honda, swirls of white vapor coming out of his mouth, the broken glass crunching under his heavy work boots. When the Honda came to a full stop, three shots blasted off in succession from its interior, ricocheting off a brick wall, the debris shattering a large glass windowpane in the office area and three of the small stained-glass windows.

"Get back in…everybody inside!" Tom Stone, the Plant Manager, yelled by the enormous gates. But Joey didn't budge. He stayed, watching the action with alert eyes, trailing Sabino, and staying within the dark skid marks left by the Honda. In the next second, he cut across, sprinting in a crouch to the employee parking lot.

Dr. Bates yelled: "Come back here, Joey!"

With a deep squint, Sabino advanced, impervious to the shots from the Honda, his silvery mane streaming with each gust of wind. Two shots whistled by Sabino's face.

"Watch out, Sabino!" exclaimed Miss Meneses, the Warehouse Master.

Fishtailing, taking the corner at the blacktop, the Honda speeded up. Joey darted out from the parked cars and leaped onto the windshield of the fleeing Honda. Dr. Bates wondered if Joey was insane. Hold on, Joey! This kid's so daring, fearless, that he borders on being irresponsible. What is he trying to prove? The masked driver rolled down his window and grabbed the kid's yellow hair to yank him off the hood, but he let go to steer back onto the blacktop.

From the opposite direction, a Peterbilt eighteen-wheeler came barreling down. The chrome of the two trumpets on top of the cabin flashed in the pale winter sunshine, plumes of black smoke swirling upward from the two upright exhaust pipes on each side of the rig. The Honda missed the semi by the width of a dime. Reaching through the driver's window, Joey snatched the mask off the driver's face as he rolled off the hood to the shoulder of the road. Taking big bumps over the shoulder of the road, the Honda got back on the blacktop and the driver speeded toward the main highway.

Joey got up, brushing his clothes off with his hands.

"You're crazy, Joey!" exclaimed Victor, picking up the ski mask.

"Have a death wish, boy?" asked Sabino. He looked at the young man for a second or two, turned around and headed back, carrying the shotgun across his chest. Victor Feng and Joey walked together behind Sabino, taking long strides toward the loading dock.

Dr. Bates watched the men's breath waft up in white quivering clouds as the wind gusts wore away. He concluded Joey was reckless or plain brave. He risked his life! Now, what makes some people brave (impelling them to take risks) and other cowards? Am I a coward? Dad and Sabino went to Vietnam when called, while others ran to Canada and Europe. Would I have gone to Vietnam or run away? He cleared his mind, for his reflections on his own frailties always put him in a foul mood.

Jossie, the supervisor of the Raw Materials Warehouse, shouted: "Way to go, Cowboy!"

Joey looked at her and winked.

"*Qué macho*! *Este chico Joey tiene muchos cojones*," said a Hispanic worker.

A crowd gathered around Joey De Lemos. Jossie, a large blond woman with braids gathered on the top of her head, asked in a loud voice: "Did you see their faces, Cowboy? Two guys, right, Joey?"

"Yeah, Jossie—a driver and the masher. They had hoods on, so I couldn't see their faces. I only saw the sideburns on one of them."

"I've got the plate numbers," said Miss Meneses.

Pointing a finger at Joey with operatic flair, Pia—the Cost Accountant—exclaimed,

"Come out of the man, thou unclean spirit!"

"Shut up, Pia," said Miss Meneses. "Get back to work!"

"All right, people. Back to work. Come on, come on, c'mon. We don't pay you to hang around here goldbricking. Let's go!" shouted Janos Panko. "Another minute and I'll dock your pay! Move it, men!" The group stirred. Janos smirked and seemed satisfied, but as the group of workers moved toward the building, a lone falsetto voice retorted,

"Go dock your mother's pay, Janos."

Dr. Bates watched Janos stand there flustered, with his mouth unhinged, fuming and furious, unable to tell the culprit. Aleksander 'Brick' Obricki, who was Janos' inseparable sidekick, said, "It came from the Analgesics group. I bet is Lenny, that mousy looking punk, but ain't sure." Brick had the build of a cinder block, not a brick; and people said that he had a puny IQ—the IQ of an ameba.

With a harsh stare and his voice thick with anger, Tom Stone—the Plant manager—addressed Joey, "I want to see you in my office in ten minutes!" To Victor: "Make sure he's there."

"Yes, sir."

Only after Tom was out of hearing range did Victor Feng open his mouth. "Tom is angry, Joey. Suppose the crooks had shot you, or maimed you, and turned you into a veggie, the company would have had to pay workers' compensation for years. The man hates that because the insurance premiums go up and…"

"Hell! My first week here," interrupted Joey, "and I'm already in trouble, man. This is the story of my life. I'm always in trouble, but all I wanted to do was help and look where it got me—I will lose my job!"

"I am afraid Tom is gonna fire you, Joey." Victor confirmed.

"You heard Tom. He put the monkey on my back, so, let's go straight to the office to wait there. We need to think of a good excuse. The way Tom looked at you reminded me of my old man and his damn switch."

# Chapter 4 — Waiting for the Worst

At the front offices of the Bates Plant, Melissa and three clerks were gossiping about the shootout and Joey's cojones when Victor and Joey walked in. Melissa, Tom B. Stone's voluptuous administrative assistant—whose speech defect amused everyone in the Plant—put her hands on her hips to scold Joey, "I just don't know about you, Joey De Lemos!"

"Please, Melissa," Victor pleaded, "Tom is going to chew his ass out. Give him a break."

"That was so-o stupid! You didn't see enough action in the Gulf War, boy? Did Saddam Hussein's nerve"—came out *nehv*—"gas get into your head?" Ignoring Victor's plea, Melissa lashed out, "Crazy—*cwayzy*—the way you chased those intruders—*intwoodehs*, and showed off. Insane is a better word." Pointing at the broken glass panel, she said, "Look what they did to the window, that beautiful stained-glass window. Now, we're going to freeze—*fweez*—our butts off until we get new glass. And where are the cops? Let me call the State cops, too." Yet, despite her tone, she flashed a flirtatious smile at Joey. Only after she turned around and bent over to unlock the low gate that marked off her office did Joey daresay,

"I was only trying to help."

Because Tom Stone kept the controlled substances in a huge walk-in freezer at the far end of Melissa's office, only Tom Stone, Sabino Yamamoto, and Dr. Bates had access. She's caged in like a canary, Joey thought. But as if the restriction was a challenge, he became even more curious, and he strained to glimpse the

Restricted area. Wondering about Melissa's age, he guessed she was in her early thirties. Look at all that wild, frizzy hair with streaks of blond. Joey couldn't resist mimicking under his breath, "Wild *fweezy heah* with *stweeks* of blond." But who's looking at her hair? That Body! Now, that's some centerfold-quality body. This Melissa is a major babe, bro! Taking a long look at Melissa's curvy body as she sashayed to her desk, swinging her hips, Joey sighed. He noted her black micro-mini skirt was riding high, and her purple blouse bulging with her high breasts. Only after he focused on the well-shaped creamy legs and the deep dimples on the back of her thighs did he feel his libido stir like a frightened fish stirs the bottom of the tank. No stockings, and that's great. She is gorgeous, exciting, and sexy. Wow, nothing like these Garden State women, a lush garden-variety. As God is truth, and as America is the Beautiful, womanhood is beauty. And the Lord God planted a garden: the Garden state! Inflamed and excited, he turned to Victor with a toothy grin.

"I'd give my eyetooth for that wholesome Jersey sweetie—a nude Jersey sweetie be even better."

When he stepped closer to the low gate, Pia—the cost accountant and self-appointed czarina of morality at the Bates Plant—darted out from her office to challenge him, "Wait a damned moment, mister! Where do you think you are going? This is a restricted area and you're not allowed to waltz in here as if you own the place."

"Sorry, Pia," said Victor. "He's new, and he still doesn't know all the rules."

"Yeah, sorry, Pia," said Joey.

"And what business do you have here if it isn't lusting after the great whore of Babylon clad in purple rags?"

Victor said, "Tom asked me and Joey to come in."

Staring at Joey and pointing an accusatory finger toward Melissa's office, she declaimed,

"And the inhabitants of the earth have been made drunk with the wine of her fornication—Revelation seventeen, verse three!"

She hooked her thumb under the right strap of her bra, snapped it loudly, and trotted off. Tapping his right temple with his right index, Victor said, "Keep your cool, bro. She is the biggest nutcase east of Eden and west of the Hudson River." He smiled and continued, "I don't believe you, Joey! Tom wants to fire you, and here you are licking your chops after 'La Monalisa.'" The Hispanic workers had nicknamed Melissa: "La Monalisa."

"Pia is right: you want to get some of that, eh?"

"Yeah, man. I rather live in sin in Cincinnati than be pious in Peoria."

They both sat down on the wooden bench and waited for Tom. "Let's face it, Joey," said Victor, "That was a macho thing to do…almost getting killed. What made you run and jump on that car? I hear you saw a lot of action with the Iraqis in the Gulf War, yet it's like you're craving for more."

"I was trying to grab the ignition keys and help."

"Listen to me, Joey. Don't lose your cool with Tom, okay? Tell him you won't do things like that anymore, that you'll think before you act—from now on. Humor the man, and that'll put Tom at ease and he won't yell at you."

"Oh, God! No yelling please," Joey said inwardly, fighting the auditory hallucination. "Stand at ease, Specialist De Lemos!" Joey heard Captain Fite yelling across the field table, his knuckles rapping the table. "You're charged with insubordination, disrespect to a noncommissioned officer, and disobeying a direct order. I will reduce your rank to the paygrade of Private First Class. If you don't agree with these charges, under the Uniform Code of Military Justice, you have a right to demand a trial by court-martial. Do you wish a court-martial? I will not allow open disregard of established authority. Do you understand?"

"I understand what you're saying, Victor," said Joey as he looked at Victor with warm eyes. "One of these days, I'll buy you a beer when we go to lunch at Daniela's place. I won't talk back to Tom. I have no beef with him; in fact, I like the man. But if somebody else pushes me around, I come out swinging. Nobody likes to be pushed around unless he's a dumb turnstile, a supermarket cart, or a lazy Susan."

"Or checkers on a board."

"Or a wheelchair."

They bumped fists, one bump up and one down.

"If you lose your job, you can stay at my place."

"Thanks, Victor—you're a good friend." But to himself, he said: "Victor is a decent man, but he isn't a relative." Alone. Not a single soul that's a blood relative. He had survived the Gulf War, but he wasn't sure about this horrible loneliness. Bummer, man. Gazing around, he noted the clerks were quiet; the stillness of the office heightening the turmoil he felt in his heart. But is Tom so unfeeling and unfair to fire a new worker for trying to help? To spend an entire lifetime dreaming and longing and praying to get a job and work here at Bates and nowhere else…and now that dream is gone. As Joey debated whether it was fair to break a worker's will and spirit to shape him to conformity, he knew he had heard Tom and Ivon and ignored them. No doubt he had disobeyed his sergeant to rescue his buddies Stuckey and Carothers—but wasn't there good in disobedience? But you can't be a free spirit if you want to keep your job. Blind obedience is the price all working stiffs have to pay to hold a job. When I was in Iraq eating bologna sandwiches full of mayonnaise and sand, he reminded himself, one hope kept me alive: That when I came back to the World, I would work for Bates. He concluded Bates was a company that cared for its workers, that the company had kept his mom at full pay because of disability. "Mom always said Bates was family," he thought.

Now, neither emboldened by his personal sense of justice, nor cowed by his doubts, but no longer upbeat, he resigned himself for the worst: to be fired.

"I hear Tom, down the hall," said Victor, turning pale, a spark of sadness in his eyes.

# Chapter 5 — Bates Headquarters

At the Hackensack MedEvac Center, Dr. Bates waited for the nurse to finish her phone call. When at last she finished, she turned and faced Dr. Bates without saying a word. Ivon explained his intention to see Lenox Davis.

"Impossible!" the nurse blurted out. "That man is in critical condition, and Doctor Spinnell left orders. The patient should rest."

Taken aback, Dr. Bates insisted but with no success, the nurse growling, "Look, mister. This is not a debating society—there's nothing I can do for you. Good day!"

Stubborn people! Insensitive, and yes, plain rude, too. Dr. Bates sighed, and with a meek expression on his face, he headed toward the exit. Scarcely was he out the door when he spun around and marched back to the station and faced the stubborn nurse.

"Let me speak to a supervisor or the head nurse," he said, finding his voice. "I'm the President of Bates Pharmaceuticals and my company gives millions of dollars to this hospital…in fact, there's a Bates ward named after my father. The least you can do…" Not waiting for him to finish his sentence, she hastened to answer, "Yes, sir. I-I'll get nurse Pritchard."

All it takes is a little gumption, nerve, and firmness. A man must speak up with authority and sound like a man—not a scary mouse. "See, now we are getting some results," he murmured. The supervisor of the Unit, nurse Pritchard, stepped out of the office and rustled to the counter, and after studying Dr. Bates for a second, she said, "I worked in the Bates Ward before I transferred here, Mr. Bates. I apologize for Violeta. She's working two back-to-back shifts, and she's now on her eighteenth hour. I'll take you to Mr. Davis' room myself."

There he is, all swaddled in gauze! Ivon saw Lenox's eyes blink with surprise and gratitude, bless his soul. Promising the company will take care of all the medical bills and that Tom will keep him on payroll at full pay regardless of what amount Workers Compensation paid him, Dr. Bates stepped closer to the bed. "And Tom will hold your job open for when your return."

"Bless you, sir."

"No, no, no sir—Ivon is fine. You've known me for over twenty years. I remember your sharing your lunch, chips, apples, and soda with me. Countless times, Lenox."

As Lenox groped for Doctor Bates' hand, his yellowish eyes filled with tears. Nurse Pritchard tore off an envelope of gauze and dabbed Lenox's eyes; and next she dabbed her own eyes. Ivon felt pleased as he thought, Everyone in the Plant will know I visited Lenox. Even Annie's eyes warmed up when she heard I was stopping here. Oh yes, this is the right move. He felt that by creating the illusion of compassion, people would like and admire him.

In the afternoon, as Victor Feng nosed the limo in front of the corner building at 57th and Eighth Avenue, Dr. Bates couldn't help noticing a change in Victor's behavior, which now showed visible nervous ticks. He saw him looking in all directions before opening the door, as if making sure no one was prowling around.

"Park and come up soon, and stop being so jumpy, because you're making me nervous—a basket case—and paranoid. We need to run a few errands this afternoon."

Going through the heavy revolving doors, Dr. Gates ambled down toward the first bank of elevators. Bates' Headquarters occupied the entire fifth floor. As the elevator reached its destination, a vague sense of panic hit him, his stomach churning. Bank loans are a pain, and the fact the bank can call them back a will—makes it worse. He felt nauseous. Victor's ticks and nervousness reminded him of Sabino's warning, and much to his surprise, his hands started trembling.

A paid murderer!

When the elevator doors slid open with a flat clang, he stood rooted to the floor for a fraction of a second. He saw the bumper-to-bumper desks and heard the din of voices mixed with the clatter of computer keyboards. Ketty Loyola—the youngest employee in the company—smiled and waved, rushing to meet him.

"You have lots of messages," said Ketty. "Your friend, Professor Dedrick, called twice. And you should listen to a weird voice-mail message saying:

'You're next—sell or die.' A distorted voice."

"Phil still around?"

"He's left for this twelve-thirty appointment at Liberty National Bank."

Ketty was a slight black-haired twenty-year-old young

woman, with a sunny disposition, who had graduated in May from Barnard College—a woman's college affiliated with Columbia University. In July, the week following old Dr. Bates' death, Phil Kerdes had hired her. During the interview Phil had elicited from her she had attended such expensive college only because her father was a handy-man in one of the college's buildings and free tuition for employees' children was one of the fringe benefits. "Of course, you still need serious volunteer work and high SATs." Since Barnard had rejected both of his daughters, the comment had mortified Phil.

Soon Ketty proved herself resourceful, becoming Ivon's ace troubleshooter. Having transformed the job of administrative assistant to that of personal executive assistant. Phil had confided to her certain weaknesses and quirks in Ivon's behavior, and had asked her to be "helpful, loving—yet firm as a mother would be with a spoiled child; Ivon's mom died when he was an infant—be discreet." Not only was Ivon pleased with her efficiency but also awed by her verbal and writing skills. And knowing that she hated Alex Panagora—having heard her refer to him as Director of Marketing and Bad Breath—Ivon felt she would spy on him, and others. Tell him rumors and inside conspiracies. Besides, she always knew what to do to draw him out of his dark, ill moods. With Ketty trailing him and reading him the messages, he no longer felt nervous as he strode to his office.

Yet he pondered about that voice-mail threat.

Two hours later, Phil Kerdes, the financial controller, walked in. Phil O. Kerdes, rumpled-suited, gaudy wide suspenders, with tufts of white and gray hair sprouting out of his ears and nose, his eyes reduced to tiny slits by the concentric circles of his thick glasses. "Matthew Metcalf's given us sixty days to pay back the loan," Phil said, coming straight to the point. "He said he couldn't extend the loan for a full year, because a committee has to approve that."

"So, we now have to start paying back this damn loan?"

Apologetic and acting as if he were to blame, Phil replied, "Unless the committee rolls it over for a year. Metcalf said that he was afraid Bates Pharmaceuticals was a 'one-man-operation,' meaning everything depended on your father's skills."

"He's right. I'm a scientist, not an administrator."

"Don't sell yourself short, Ivon. You need a little experience—that's all. A few months on the job and you will outshine any MBA if you set your mind to it. You've got brains. Your father didn't have a business degree and look what he accomplished in both fields, research and business."

"I want to stay out of the way, keep a low profile; maybe this death threat will blow away. Let's talk about a headhunter, someone with computer skills and finance savvy, someone with experience in private placements on Wall Street." With a fearful look, Dr. Bates looked at Phil.

"I don't know what to do, Phil. I'm scared. Sabino says that I should keep my eyes open. He's afraid the people who killed my father will come after me…and it seems they are. Someone left this voice-mail threat. I'm trying not to think about it, but I'm worried. You feel the same way, don't you, Phil—that a killer is out to get me?"

Phil said, "Detective Wilkins is sure one of those companies that made offers to buy us out is behind it. He also suspects Alex, since it's well known that Alex wants to be President of the company. That pompous Aussie has ambitions!"

"Sabino says he's convinced Helen McCain's behind it. You know, Orbis has grown because of mergers, acquisitions, and leveraged buyouts."

"Detective Wilkins says everything points to Peter Rashkin, Orbis' former chief of security. But this Rashkin has disappeared with no trace—totally vanished. Anyway, the good detective will tell us what he has learned so far on Monday."

Ivon changed the subject, "Union organizers are acting up again at the plant."

Startled by a loud knock on the door, Ivon paled. Alex Panagora, the Director of Sales, Marketing, and Public Relations, swirled in, "Ivon, we have to talk. We can't allow the company to drift without *direcchaon*. You know your *fawther* built the *companee*, but I made it a *shuparior companee…*"

"Sure, Alex. We'll talk in a few days…"

"Look, son. I have no *toim* to spare now, but ye need to hear some *oideas* I have. Phillip? See that Ivon fixes a *toim* for the three of us to meet? Tell Myrna or call me on my cell phone—but let's talk, son. I mean soon. *Toim* is of the *oisense*."

"Sure, Alex. You're right. I'm sorry I haven't talked with you…but, the police investigation, problems at the Plant, one headache after the other…" To which Alex made a sour face, turning around, and leaving with the same abruptness as he had coming in.

Phil stared at Ivon with a hurt look on his face that all but declared, "Don't let Alex talk to you as if you were his son. Whether he likes it or not, you're the boss, Ivon. He'll walk all over you if you let him."

Placing his hand on Phil's shoulder, Ivon said, "Let's continue this discussion on Monday." Sensing what was on Phil's mind, he added, "Alex has known me since I was a teenager, and I guess he still sees me as a kid. It'll take some time for him to accept me as the President of the company." Ivon placed his hand on Phil's shoulder and walked him to the door. "Now, get me a copy of the Capital Budget you and dad worked. I want to get cracking with that new equipment."

Mocking Alex's accent, Phil said, "I'll be *deloited* to, *moit.*"

Once at his desk, Ivon called Tom Stone at the plant. Tom told him that the police had found the Honda on a side street in Union City. Of course, the car turned out to be stolen. They agreed to discuss the Union problem in person the following week.

Ketty came in. "Victor is outside." "Ask him to wait five more minutes."

After Ketty left, Dr. Bates called Cecilia Van Osburgh—who had been old Dr. Bates' companion, and a surrogate mother to young Doctor Bates—inviting her to a concert and dinner, to which Cecilia agreed. Cecilia was the sole owner of a private equity company, and the heir of vast holdings in real estate and financial assets. As Bates Pharmaceuticals grew, Cecilia injected fresh capital into the company.

When Victor came in, Ivon said, "We need to go book shopping at Barnes and Noble." During his student years at Yale and MIT, Dr. Bates had avoided, even derided, business courses, but he now saw the need to read up to fill the vacuum. That same afternoon Ivon and Victor visited the Barnes and Noble store on the corner of 83rd Street and Broadway. Dr. Bates filled two blue baskets with "How To" books: *The ABCs of Accounting, How to Analyze Financial Statements in One Hour, Cash Flows Statements*

*Made Easy,* and other similar titles he thought useful. On the first floor, right in the center of the store, Dr. Bates saw a book by the Mexican poet Octavio Paz, *The Double Flame: Love and Eroticism.* Go for it, Octavio! Tossing the book in his basket, hoping he could learn something about love, to find a hidden snippet that'd stir his heart and mind, to find a seed of wisdom to grow in both mind and heart. Oh, yes, Plato, Stendhal, Ortega, and the great poets—Ah! Dante, Milton, Shakespeare, Petrarch, Neruda—in the end, they all fail. And they fail because their showy and sweet words drain rather than fill, stunt rather than sprout. Humans need plain, sweet love that is undisputable, yet they supply no lasting image of what love is. Poets, he felt, have opinions about the eternal enigmas: being and becoming, permanency and change, stillness and flux. But the fundamental question is: what is the unmoved substance that nurtures love in all its forms? I am only twenty-five years old. I will wait and search for an answer, for love brings happiness to life and life to happiness.

Next, they stopped at a software store where Dr. Bates picked up a Windows update, Quicken for Windows, the McAfee Virus Scan program, and a Parallel-port Laplink cable. As they rode south on Broadway, Victor said, "I'm computer-illiterate, but my nephew Marcus is a whiz, a computer science major at NYU and an Internet freak or geek. Number one hacker! He was in a Chinatown gang before I pushed him to go to college."

Soon they saw a traffic jam up ahead at 60th Street. "Let me out, Victor," Ivon said. "I'll walk to the office from here; come back before seven. We'll pick up Cecilia before seven thirty at Sutton Place. Tonight, we're going to Alice Tully Hall for a chamber music concert—at Lincoln Center."

Taking long strides, with that distinctive awkward gait, as though his knees were slipping and grating, Dr. Bates hurried along Broadway. The price you must pay for three years of grueling Ivy League basketball competition. Playing Center for the Yale Bulldogs varsity team had not been a cakewalk. And since the school did not allow freshmen to play varsity basketball, he had joined the boxing and Greco-Roman wrestling teams. There you have it, a nose broken four different times: once in a tough sparring session, and three times in basketball by flying elbows.

In front of the New York Coliseum, he saw a middle-aged

couple—foreign tourists, husband and wife from the Middle East, Dr. Bates thought—pointing at the Columbus statue. The wife started snapping pictures. To the side of the couple, he saw two mounted police officers talking to a large, hulking man who was asking for directions.

A bearded, seedy homeless man ran to the woman and yelled, "Goddamn Arab spies! You steal our atomic secrets and smuggle out our property, too." The madman stepped up to the couple and barked, "Rotten terrorists!"

When the husband spoke to his wife in Arabic, the bum shrieked and cursed, yanking the woman's hair from side to side. The stunned woman started screaming at the top of her voice. Despite his size—since he was a potbellied, small-boned man—the furious husband shoved the man with force. The bum crashed against a pile of bulging bags piled around a cracked and drippy fire hydrant. Frozen, Dr. Bates didn't know what to do amid all the confusion. Although he felt he needed to do something, he was hesitant whether to help the couple, restrain the madman or leave. Instead, he said to the two leather-jacketed mounted police officers, "Get off your horses and help these people!" Spurring the horses onto the sidewalk, the cops frightened the bum and three homeless women followed him toward the Maine Memorial entrance to Central Park. The two Horse-cops circled away, their light blue helmets with dark visors glimmering. Noticing the homeless women, Doctor Bates thought, We see homeless and mad people everywhere, even in nightmares! But why didn't he help the couple?

The husband, a frail man, did not hesitate at all; he defended his woman with honor and nobility.

As he replayed the scene, he felt annoyed with himself and soon he felt depressed and wanted to go home, curl up in bed, put on his robe and hide. Once at the office, he tried to read the book on cash flows. Neither great effort nor steady concentration helped. These cash flow statements are not for civilians! Slamming the book down in irritation, he uttered: "Mr. Phil O. Kerdes will have to give me a simple explanation that makes sense, one with no mumble of jumbo or jargon."

Suddenly, an odd thought formed in his mind, and his stomach rolled in fear.

"Wait a minute!" he exclaimed. "That hulking man talking to the cops…is the same man who was browsing at Barnes & Noble. Is this a coincidence? No way!"

He realized the man was following him! Soon a deep chill spread over his body, and for a second—which seemed an eternity—he felt petrified. That guy is after me! A paid assassin is after me. He shifted in his chair and said, "I know why I didn't help that couple, and I know why I am so nervous: I am a coward!" His long arms fell over the sides of his chair, and he slouched, all energy draining from his body. A gloomy foreboding twisted inside him like a black ink-soaked rag. He fought the hurt of being a spineless dud in vain; in vain, he tried to divert his attention and think of other thoughts, and try hard as he might, he could not.

After a long while, the drumming at the door drew him from the black torpor that had suffused him. He heard Ketty come around the desk and say, "Oh, Ivon—you're brooding! You have ten minutes to get ready, or you'll miss the concert." Prancing to the closet, she brought out fresh underwear and a wine-red terry robe, rushed to the far wing of the office to set the items on a tray by the sauna-shower room, nudging him toward the shower. As he undressed and trudged to the shower, Ketty returned to the closet to draw a charcoal-dark suit, a white shirt, and a fresh, quiet paisley tie.

Cheered by Ketty's solicitude and nurse-like aplomb, he now looked forward to seeing Cecilia and going to the concert. He thought he'd be safe at Lincoln Center, where there's much security; no one would try anything there. He heard Ketty's voice through the roar of the shower. "Your tickets are for Alice Tully Hall—where the Chamber Music Society performs, not Avery Fisher Hall. They're in the inside pocket—don't take too long. Victor is waiting outside."

# Chapter 6 — The Istanbul Boutique

Because his instincts never betrayed him as soon as Joey saw Tom Stone's eyes, he knew he was safe; that he wasn't firing him. What is it with Tom that is so warm and human? Of course, he's tough; no matter, he's a loving, sweet man. Still, Joey De Lemos received a scathing reprimand for chasing the thugs. "What the hell were you trying to prove, son? This is a warning. No more screw-ups, or your ass will be out on the street! Either you shape up or you ship out." Tom spoke to him with a harsh tone, and if not cruel or mean, at least not mild nor affable.

"No, sir. Everything is cool." *Thank you Lord.*

Since every Friday was payday at the Bates plant, when Joey got his paycheck, he asked Tom Stone for permission to leave at 3 p.m. to open a bank account in Union City. Tom agreed, urging him to stay out of trouble. At half-past three, Cowboy drove his souped-up 1959 Impala hardtop into the bank's parking lot behind the building. Place's packed! That spot looks tight, but with a strong wrist the mighty-winged Impala—a survivor of many drag strip races in and around Leonia, Fort Lee, Englewood, Hackensack, Bogota, and other back-water towns—will go in. And so it did. Entering the bank through the back door that fronted the parking lot, he saw a bustling bay and decided not to stay.

Too crowded, man.

Sauntering out the front door to Bergenline Avenue, he crossed the avenue at the busy stoplight by the new Burger King, edging along a narrow alley. He rang the bell of the Istanbul Boutique. The attendant, who was showing some posters to a group of noisy customers, let him in.

"More posters," said the young woman, raising her voice and pointing toward the west wall of the store, "by the jewelry section. Jerry Garcia and Sting are back there—we still have a few left."

Without embarrassing her, he eyed her. What's she wearing? Hmm, black stretch pants and a suede sleeveless vest unbuttoned in the front—and that matching bra lifting her breasts in undulating curves. He saw that a long-toothed barrette was holding her plentiful brown hair gathered on top. As soon as the raucous group left, he stepped close to her and soon he was admiring the rings on her fingers, caressing her hand. Stretching across the counter, he nibbled at her right ear, from which at least half a dozen silver rings hung.

The girl jerked back. "Don't get too fresh. My boyfriend is in the back and he gets nasty sometimes. The jerk."

Leaning over the counter and with trembling lips, he kissed her gold nose-stud. If she didn't have that grinding sadness in her eyes, she'd be a sexy doll. Fine, full lips. Fine, full breasts. What she ought to do is get rid of that boyfriend. The glitter of a chromed.38 revolver that was on display to the right of the register caught his eye.

"Show me that gun."

"It's a magician's gun, a real look-alike." She chose a key from a huge jangling ring holder and unlocked the sliding door, bringing the gun out with an anxious look on her face.

Cocking the gun and aiming it at the lit candle skull, which was burning and filling the store with a sweet-acrid scent, on the wall shelf, he squinted his left eye, squeezing the trigger. But instead of hearing the metallic click, he heard a loud explosion, which left his ears ringing. The young woman's face turned white like Greek yogurt. From the backroom, three guys came rushing out, scanning with cautious eyes, and behind them a fourth guy floating in slow motion.

"The damned thing had a blank in the chamber," said Cowboy with a sheepish grin.

"Scared the hell outta me!" said the short plump man, the owner of the store. "Lisa, I've told you many times to call me when a customer wants to look at an item that's priced fifty and above. You don't know how to sell this merchandise and I lose the sale."

"It's my fault," said Cowboy. "I wanted to try it out."

"You don't look like no magician to me," said Lisa's boyfriend, in a whiny, sniveling voice.

Dion Loco Bromius—the boyfriend—was wearing black jeans, a black shirt, and a black leather jacket with chains and leather cap, a Confederate cap; cocked to one side. He was a tall, cruel-eyed man with a menacing stare who walked with a slight limp.

Taking an instant dislike to Cowboy, Dion Loco Bromius' icy stare as much as said, "Better watch your ass, punk!" He shifted his gaze from Lisa to the blond kid, the light in his eyes showing a jealous streak. After a quick look at Lisa, he eased off with a smirk of nervous satisfaction.

"He looks more like a cowboy to me," said the skin-headed fat guy who was wearing a black Tommy Hilfiger T-shirt much too short to cover his enormous stomach. Cowboy noticed that both of the man's forearms covered with tattoos: Nazi crosses, Viking swords, skulls, coiled snakes, roses, and right smack on his biceps, inside a circle, three blocked letters: WSP—white supremacist power.

Looking at the floating fourth guy, whose eyes were half-shut, his head bobbing, Cowboy said, "My man's stoned out of his mind! Homeboy is rocking."

"My name is Lou," said the owner, offering his hand in a gesture of trust. "I have superior stuff in the back, not your regular Colombian grass, but top-grade Asian weed from Thailand. Let's have us a couple of good hits."

Dion Loco Bromius screamed, "Let's rock'n roll, smoke and roll!" Skinhead squealed. "You roll, Loco. I've got my pipe."

"Yeah man," they all chimed in a chorus with a thrill of anticipation, except for the space cadet who was still out in far orbit. They marched single file into the backroom, a room cramped with pipes, scales, clear plastic bags and other smoking paraphernalia. A metal desk and a chair took up half of the space. On the wall, in front of the desk, a guitar hung on a large nail; Cowboy sat on the floor since there was only one chair and one stool. A thick haze hung in the room like a giant, steamy mushroom.

Dion Loco Bromius whined about his unemployment checks running out and all the jobs going across the border to Mexico and to Taiwan and South Korea, "and what we Americans are gonna do about it?"

"Damn Mexicans, Koreans, and other chinks," said Skinhead, "are like elephants—they work for peanuts."

"Yeah," complained Dion Loco Bromius, "they are taking all the jobs away from us Americans. Look at me. While I'm unemployed them wetbacks and yellowbellies have jobs. Is anybody in Washington doing something about it? Nah! Nothing. Nada!"

Smoking for a while and teasing one another, they let the Thai cannabis weed transport them in rapturous flight. A weed riled Loco

Bromius started razzing Cowboy, "That rat-tail of yours doesn't look too cool, my man…it only looks good on dark-haired people."

The skin-headed fat man—Hog, remarked that it looked okay to him and that Cowboy was a fine specimen of the superior white Aryan race. Lou teased, "Wanna go steady with him Hog?" Some hooting followed. Hog laughed with a peal of childlike laughter.

After a while Cowboy fixed his eyes on the guitar, and saw the guitar was yawning and melting, man. A while later, Lisa stuck her head in with a harried look on her face: "Lou, I need help in the front—store's packed." Bolting to his feet, Lou hurried out, returning within a few minutes to warn them, "Now you cool it, guys. Don't light up anymore, okay? Dion, Hog, open some windows, man; the smell's all over the front! As soon as I have a chance, I'll order some Chinese food."

Thirty minutes later, Lou returned carrying two bags with Chinese food, Lisa trailing him, dragging a bag bulging with several six-packs of beer.

"Thank you, Lisa," said Hog as he grabbed a stack of paper plates from a shelf. "You're a walking contradiction, Hog," said Lisa. "Those tattoos don't match your heart. You're kind and sweet and gentle and I've never seen you hurt anyone. Why do you act tough?"

"The weak are always poor and the rich tough. I wanna be rich one day."

"He is a retard!" said Dion Loco Bromius. "Born a retard, always a retard. Ain't but one thing that Hog knows, and that is to eat. Chow time, men!"

As they inhaled the food, Lou explained how a few years back he had bought one thousand Jerry Garcia posters at twenty cents each, and now they're going at ten dollars a shot, my man. Cowboy agreed with a nod that Lou had a magic touch for making money. What's Hog eyeing? Oh yes, the half-eaten egg roll! He's still hungry, even though he's polished off his plate. "Here, Hog," said Cowboy, "want it?" Satisfied, they talked and kidded around for a while. Homeboy—now clear-eyed, free of hunger pangs, and clear-headed—picked up the guitar and started strumming a few chords, getting the feel of it. He switched the tempo and with two or three basic triads on the upper frets, he accompanied himself to a mournful rhythm-and-blues song:

Rolling stones gather no guilt

I can see no sin on the riverbed

The cramped, seedy room filled up and resonated with the sweetest and most angelic tenor voice Cowboy had ever heard in his twenty-three years. He felt immersed in a strange bliss. Is it the cannabis weed? Maybe it's the melody, or the lyrics, or the sentiment in Homeboy's voice, or perhaps memories that cause this feeling. Soon he was dancing and laughing, faint and light-headed, the room shimmering with brilliant happy hues. I've always been on the outside looking in, but not now—this bliss is within!

But not for long, for with half-lidded eyes he watched Dion Loco Bromius pull a switchblade, click it open and twirl it a few times.

Homeboy stopped singing. Hog scooted.

Cowboy felt a shadow pass over the room, slam against the wall, and hang on to the nail where the guitar had been hanging a moment ago, danger and violence now weighing down the rusty spike. "Hang there, man," he murmured.

The small room fell silent. "I g-gotta go, Lou," stuttered Loco. "You sing well, and all that, Homeboy, but this ain't my kind of music. I go for Bloody Metal, man." With practiced skill, Loco twirled the blade; switching it between hands, "Let's mix some bleer." Pressing the sharp blade over his forearm, stuck it in and a trickle of blood wrapped around his wrist, dripping into his can of beer.

Rising to his feet, he guzzled down the bleer, mashing the can against his forehead, dropping the flattened can to the floor. "I'm going to Donato's. My man Donato is wise and learned, and never bores you, like you turkeys bore me now. He talks to you about almost anything in the world since he's traveled the four continents and all them seas—wanna come along, Hog?"

"I'm staying," replied Hog.

Sneering and fixing a threatening stare on Cowboy, Loco said, "Somehow, I got the feeling I am gonna see you around, my man—like this isn't the last time we cross paths. Dunno why. Fact is, I got this rotten feeling about you." He strode off, leaving a streak of rank body odor behind him.

Not one to run from confrontation, Joey struggled to keep quiet.

Only after Dion was gone did they resume their talk. Lou said, "If Loco likes blood so much, he should come back as a used tampon in his next life, like that turkey, Prince Charles. Since Loco started hanging around that preacher Donato, his whole life has changed. Not that he was a saint. He was always cruel and mean, but now he's close to being a psychopath. I hear they have midnight masses and crap like that in that church. Bad vibes, man. I hear rumors that Donato wanted to build a church in Delphi, outside the Bates Plant, but that Sabino chased him out. Anyway, what's bad is that Donato is attracting more and more followers every day."

A strange feeling of loneliness and dread gripped Cowboy's heart. Or was it fear? The deranged Dion Loco Bromius may be waiting outside, may be stalking him. He saw him attacking him, stabbing him from behind, Loco's blade cutting, scratching between two ribs and sinking into his right lung. Arching his back, he screamed, but he didn't hear his voice. Instead, he heard Hog say, "Don't worry, Cowboy. Loco was only trying to scare you—he senses Lisa likes you. He's more jealous than Hotelo."

Lou Smiled, "You mean Othello, Hog."

Cowboy again wondered if Loco was waiting for him outside. Pondering why Loco had taken such a deep dislike to him, such animosity, the thought crossing his mind that perhaps Loco was a bizarre, distorted image of his own wicked self. His double. Why, he even looks like mom. Always on the outside looking in, never fitting in, and not by design but by choice. Was meeting Loco Bromius an accident of fate? At any rate, he was alone in this world and he missed his mother, for he'd never met his father, and more than anything in the world, he wished he had. He thought I must find him! I can't go through life with this damn feeling that causes loneliness and insecurity—bummer, man. He felt like an orphan in a senseless, crippling universe that cares less if one dies or lives. Some people walk around with holes in their soles and others with holes in their souls. What tormented him daily was that while in the war he had comforted others in their moments of death, he'd been absent from his own mother's deathbed. She'd died alone, man. I feel like a cowboy riding by his lonesome self on a lame horse called Remorse.

Burying his head in his arms so that the others wouldn't see that he was weeping, he thought, "Jesus wept, and he knew why…He redeemed people and wept bitterly because he also redeemed the bad people, too. Not just the good ones. But I don't know why." And though he went on weeping, he also wanted to scream.

# Chapter 7 — Sell or Die

While they waited in the lobby of Alice Tully Hall at Lincoln Center until the pre-concert talk was over, Cecilia commented, “I thought people who came to the Chamber Music Society concerts were older people like me; I never paid attention before. Look at all the handsome young people!”

“Ivon Bates! Is that you?” They heard a rushed voice.

A young brunette in a Valentino business suit steered her companion, a dainty woman with a Peter Pan look, to where Dr. Bates and Cecilia were standing; the brunette’s attractiveness drawing admiring stares from the crowd.

“Laura…Laura Standish, what a delightful surprise,” said Dr. Bates.

Handling the introductions with grace, Laura set everyone at ease. “I’m with Brooke, Sterne, and Benz,” said Laura, “the Investment Bankers. I heard you went to MIT, but I came to the Big Apple to get a *juris* and an MBA from Columbia. Irene has been doing some research for an article and she tells me you are the heir of Bates…of Bates Pharmaceuticals!”

Cecilia smiled. “Ivon is now the owner and the new chief executive officer,” she said and added with a tone of pride in her voice, “He’s taken over the reins of the company.”

“Isn’t it uncanny?” asked Laura. “Irene was telling me about Bates Pharmaceuticals, its low profile, and how little anybody knew about the company until Dr. Bates was…your father was…I’m sorry, Ivon, I didn’t mean to bring…”

“No, no, it’s okay, Laura,” said Dr. Bates.

Laura continued, “Irene writes for the Wall Street Journal and she wants to do a piece about your company.”

Tugging at Dr. Bates’ sleeve, Irene Cohen said, “Ivon, you must let me interview you. Please. This is going to be a big break for your company…and me, of course. I beg you.”

Neither agreeing nor disagreeing, Dr. Bates remained silent. As the bells announced the concert was starting in three minutes, the ushers urged the patrons to their seats.

Ivon said, “Listen Laura, why don’t we get together sometime next week? Let’s the three of us get together. Is that all right, Laura? Irene?”

"I'll call your office, Ivon," said Laura. "Is Cassandra in Manhattan, too? Or did she go back to Ithaca?"

Taken aback, Dr. Bates hesitated for a second. Oh, you innocent sweetheart! Must you pour salt on an open wound?

"She's from Troy—not Ithaca. She's back in Troy."

As they found their seats Cecilia said, "Think of me as a paranoid old cranky dowager, but I think that was no chance encounter, Ivon. That young woman has an angle. I've got the strange feeling that she was stalking you!"

"I'd wish! When we were at Yale, Laura ran around with the IRS."

"You mean studying to be an IRS agent?"

"No, Cecilia. IRS is the euphemism the frat boys use for the Immensely Rich Set. Isn't she a lovely young woman?"

Cecilia said. "A gorgeous and perfect beauty she is—but a perfection that destroys."

"I think you will like her."

"And I suppose, Cassandra—how à propos that she is from Troy—is the bimbo you ran around with for a while? I am glad that's over with. Good riddance!"

During the concert, Dr. Bates would steal a look at Cecilia, who was a beauty to behold despite the ravages of age, since she now was in her mid-fifties. And tonight, she wore a brown wool coat and pants, and a tasteful apricot blouse, with a high-winged collar. She wore no jewelry other than two diamond studs in her small ears. Her plentiful hair—a natural salt and pepper mane — swept back and tied in a bun held by a black bow. Cecilia Van Osburgh, one of the wealthiest ladies in Manhattan, renowned scholar, disciple of Meyer Schapiro, the legendary Professor of Fine Arts at Columbia University. She spoke several Romance languages plus perfect German and Dutch.

Ivon recalled seeing on the shelf next to her night table several editions in assorted languages of Cervantes's *Don Quijote*, Garcia Marquez's *One Hundred Years of Solitude*, Lacan's *Ecrits*, Octavio Paz's *Complete Poems*, and Borges' *Fictions,* and of late, a translation of Murakami's *The Wind-Up Bird Chronicle*. His early childhood memories were the adventures of Sancho and Don Quijote that Cecilia had read to him.

To their delight, the program had been superb: Debussy,

Messiaen, and Takemitsu, a Japanese composer with whom they were both unfamiliar, but who turned out to be a most pleasant surprise. Cecilia had pointed out to Dr. Bates Takemitsu's moving melancholy silences, "Reminds me of T. S. Eliot: at the still point of the turning world," she had whispered to Ivon, "at the still point, there the dance is."

"Still point, still point," murmured Ivon, as if trying to pierce the veneer of the words to touch some raw, unmediated meaning. As he rode back to his apartment, he thought about Cassandra. Beethoven's piano Sonata No. 25 played in his mind. Ah, the Sonatina! Cassandra would spend hours practicing it, going over the third movement again and again. Cassandra, Cass, Cassie, fuel of my fire. He saw her nude at the Steinway—left hand crossing over the right—fingers flying over the keyboard, her full round breasts rising, cleaving, and pushing together.

But his recollection was brief, for his mind shifted to the Plant, to the labs, as Cassandra's image morphed into that of Dr. Annie G. Norris. He felt tinglish and warm as he pictured and beheld Annie's fresh, wide smile. He held the image at length, enjoying its pure, virginal glow. Much to his chagrin, Joey De Lemos' face replaced Annie's, seeing him walking as a point man and sniffing out an ambush, urging his men to take cover and return fire. I wonder who this young man—Joey De Lemos—reminds me of. Who are his parents? Where does he come from? He suspected that Tom Stone knew something about Joey and that Tom wasn't sharing the secret with anyone. He asked Ketty to poke around, to talk to Melissa La Monalisa; a little sleuthing would not hurt.

He awoke to an apartment redolent of Colombian coffee, frying bacon, eggs, and the distinct aroma of Pillsbury cinnamon rolls flowing from the oven. Antonia—Ivon's housekeeper, cook, beloved nanny-mother figure—was singing and fussing in the kitchen. After a hot shower, he put on a sweat suit, the top of which sported three large block letters: MIT. Sneaking into the kitchen, he tried to steal a strip of bacon, but Antonia caught him and slapped his hand. "You mind? —*jiu mine*?—You *seet*, I *brrreeeng*, *den* you *eet*, okay? You no ask…and *das* no good! ¡Que muchacho tan loco que no tiene maneras!

Antonia raised Ivon since he was five years, indulging and spoiling him to no end. She also cleaned Cecilia's apartment. The bond between Ivon and Antonia was as strong as the bond he felt for Cecilia, having grown up calling Cecilia mom and Antonia mamá. Only after he was in his early teens did he start calling them by their first name; after they explained to him that neither of them was his natural mother; that his mother had died, leaving him in their care.

Little Ivon would often question them about his actual mother but never got a straightforward answer, which over the years grew into an obsession with learning the truth.

After he read the Sunday Times, he dressed and went to attend the 11 a.m. service at Rutgers Presbyterian Church on West 73rd. Before he left he pointed to the old computer set and told Antonia, "You take it home. It is still a good computer; give it to Lola."

Antonia eyes lit up, "Ah *si*! *Gracias, mi Nino*."

In the evening he watched "60 Minutes," at the end of which he clicked off the TV set and ambled to the stereo. Removing from the CD player the two volumes of Julio Iglesias's In Concert, that Antonia loved and his own choice from the previous night: Billy Joel's Greatest Hits. He replaced them with Bach's Brandenburg Concertos, Mendelssohn's Octet, and Dawn Upshaw's I Wish It So. Gazing at the glimmering trophies that crowded a large section of the teak wall unit, he thought, those were wonderful years, carefree years, free from any danger. The bright, effulgent, tiny sphere that seemed out of place among the trophies caught his eye. A shiver ran down his spine as he relived the instant when Sabino had placed the sphere in his hand. It is even smaller than the tip of my pinky! It's so bright, Sabino, it hurts my eyes! How old was he then? Five, maybe? Oh, yes! He saw the swamp, the grove of majestic, ancient cedars that seemed to touch the clouds, and right there in their midst, Sabino's twitching eagle-eye had spotted the mysterious tiny rock.

Listening to the violin, oboes, horns, and bassoons blending into the allegro cadences of Brandenburg concerto No. 1, Dr. Bates picked up Octavio Paz's book, *The Double Flame: Love and Eroticism* and opened it at random. But instead of reading, his mind's eye saw Cassandra floating at the small party his advisors and friends threw for him after he defended his doctoral dissertation. And later, their happy days together. Her white-blond hair glinting in the sun and her large breasts moist with perspiration and how he loved to watch her play the piano—naked, of course! And what a thrill to see her and to hear her play the Sonatina's third movement!

"Watch this, Ivon," she'd call, her powerful fingers hammering the keyboard. He'd stand behind her, cup her full ivory-white breasts, and kiss her neck, and their sweaty bodies would fuse in a passionate pretzel. But he also heard her bossy and haughty voice: "If this is the life of a scientific researcher…it's bo-o-ring. And for what? Ivon, you earn less money than an assistant professor!"

With modesty—but not without sincerity—Ivon had offered, "Let's move to New York City. My dad owns this small company and even though I…"

"Yes, you've told me, a small factory that makes shampoos, shoe polish, and soaps. Thanks, but no thanks!"

But the giggle, the breathless laughter, and the insipid voice—Who's you? — he'd overheard on the other side of the door jolted him from his reverie. When he returned from his father's funeral, he ended their relationship.

After reading a few pages of Paz's book, he tossed the book; he had expected to find a humble formula for love, and instead, he found an eloquent philosophical disquisition about it. To think one can find love in a book! A faint noise by the front door caught his attention. Next, he heard more insisting scratching at the door. Is it the front door? A night visitor? He rose to his feet, his pulse racing with quiet alertness, his ear cocked. Or did it come from the kitchen? No, no. Someone's turning the front doorknob. Ice ran through his veins.

The paid assassin!

Gathering courage, he skulked to the door, where—after taking a deep breath—he yanked it open. But no one was there. His eyes darted to the floor.

Ah, a note!

Picking up the piece of paper, he read the message printed with a felt-tip pen: SELL OR DIE. Fear over-brimmed his heart. Double bolting the door, he turned the lights off and raced to the front window to glimpse the messenger, but he only saw—in the penumbra, to the side of the ill-lit sign of the all-night diner—three grotesque women hooded and huddled against the wind. The street was desolate and dim, the asphalt and lights garbed with a foggy, gloomy veil. Now he felt frightened, and utterly alone. As he pondered Cassandra's words, *You will lose…the laurel, the trunk, the plant, and the offshoots: an evil seed and a good seed.* He could discern no clue. When faced with danger, why is the need for a blood relative so deep in the human beast? When he felt most vulnerable, he'd appeal to his best comfort: the Friars and Monks tunic. Drawing the tunic—coarse, red-wine hued—from the chest of drawers and cradling it to his face, he sniffed it. He snapped it open and was about to put it on, but he abruptly changed his mind, putting it back in the drawer. No, a man has to be brave—no time for sophomoric props. I must learn to be brave. I can't go through life being a coward. He donned a set of cotton pajamas and hopped into the cool sheets, his fevered mind pondering the dilemma—to be or not to be: sell and stay alive, or keep the company and risk death. What counted, he decided, was to stay alive.

# Chapter 8 — Orbis Security

Slamming the telephone down, Helen McCain cursed, "Damned cob-knocker! This guy Devlin is an incompetent fool who is letting things get out of control. A fine way to start the week! Listening to the babblings of a crybaby; he's a useless dunce to be sure." Since this was the third time burglars hit the Plant this year, McCain asked Camilla to call Lester Lowmax to tell him she'd be down to see him shortly to discuss the matter.

Walking into the Control Room, she saw that Lester Lowmax was conducting a workshop: an earphone and a lip mike were barely visible on his face. When Lowmax saw her, he removed the devices, but McCain stopped him.

"No, no, go on, Lester. I'll watch for a while."

"The heart of the system is on the third tier: the Operations Panel," continued Lowmax. McCain saw two hair-thin wires with earphones lying flat on the marble top of the station. Damn wires look like pubic hairs! Oh, Lester the Molester, aren't you a smug, melon-headed show off? All at once, monitor D3 started beeping and flashing a warning signal. Lowmax zoomed in and the large screen flooded with the images of a messenger wearing a bicycle helmet, spandex pants, and a large bag slung over his shoulder. With quick fingers Lowmax typed commands and pushed buttons.

Next, Lowmax's baritone voice boomed through the speakers: "Detain messenger coming out of elevator 8. Repeat. Detain messenger coming out of elevator 8. Suspect is wearing a bicycle helmet and tight stretch pants."

Captain Beasley, the Chief's second in command, stepped up closer to the monitors. To his right stood Lieutenant Wesley, the Chief of Plant Security, and Sergeant Freddy Morales, while others quickly clustered around them to watch the action on the monitors that were displaying the lobby from various angles. They saw the doors of elevator 8 open, and right outside, two tall men in dark suits stood glaring and blocking the way. The messenger's left elbow sprung like an exploding piston, hitting the man to his left in the ribs, shoving the other man hard, catching him off-guard and sending him to the floor. Unimpeded, the messenger ran toward the south revolving door, clutching his bag tight against his side, his spindly legs flying.

"Stop that man!"

Were it not for the uniformed guard stationed by the north revolving door, the man would have escaped. Seizing the messenger by the neck, the guard picked a swift chop to the man's clavicle bone, causing the man to collapse in a heap.

Watching the screen closely, Helen McCain's eyes shone with perverse delight.

Lowmax said, "Did you see that? Is that the new hire?"

"That's Orlando—my new rookie," said Captain Beasley. "he passed his polygraph exam with flying colors and just completed his two weeks of training."

"Excellent choice, Zach." Chief Lowmax then ordered, "Zach, take a uniform with you and bring that clown to me."

Staring at Beasley, Helen McCain wondered why Zach Beasley had no eye-brows. What a weird man! He looks like a thick-necked ape with a shaven head and get a load of those folds in the back of his neck—like a roller blader just run over it leaving those two deep creases.

A few minutes later, Zach Beasley returned to the Panopticon—a name that Chief Lowmax loved to use for his control room—with the messenger. Lowmax addressed the detainee,

"All I want is some honest answers. If you tell me the truth, nothing will happen to you. If you lie…well, that's your choice. Old Zach's brother was killed by one of your kind a while back, and he's still grieving."

The messenger looked at Beasley, and he broke out sobbing.

"Empty all your pockets." The bag had a tool belt sewn against one of its sides, and in the grooves, they could see pliers, wire cutters, screwdrivers, box cutters, tension scissors, and wrenches of all sizes. Pointing at the Laptop half-hidden in the bag,

Lowmax said, "This computer belongs to our Senior V.P. Henry Cook — what the hell are you doing with it?" He turned to Beasley. "Zach, you know the procedure…get him out of here! When you are done with him, you and Morales report to my office. We got serious business to attend to: a Jersey assignment for you."

"This is very heartening, Lester! That is what I call fine security. I hate to see intruders walking around the building unchallenged," said Helen McCain. Never had she felt so secure in the building as now.

"You wanna see Captain Beasley's interrogation techniques?"

Knowing that Beasley was a cruel man, she declined. He's a monster; but what is a monster but a man with a barren soul? I know better than anyone else—I loved one: Joe Bates. But let's not obsess about monsters or I could turn into one. He he he.

Lowmax escorted McCain to the elevators. Yes, of course she was concerned about the break-in at the Long Island City plant. "God forbid they find and steal the controlled substances!" she warned Lowmax. Certainly, she wanted Lowmax to get started with the Bates Pharmaceuticals project. The icy tone in her voice alarmed Lowmax, who read the scowl on her faced as an unsaid warning, "I am tired of all this boring talk. It is high time to act and you, my friend, must get me some results."

McCain said, "I have to attend a manufacturers' convention in Wichita Falls and then testify in Washington, so when I return next week, I expect you to have some intelligence and a preliminary plan, Lester. Time's not on our side."

As she trundled down toward the elevators, her mind was full of insistent mental chatter: Why steal *that* laptop? Henry the Eight's Laptop? Of course, he keeps tons of confidential data. Can you imagine all that data in our enemy's hands? Then, a sensation in her stomach traveled to her mind, setting off an alarm. Something didn't add up: the messenger had white teeth, polished teeth, well cared for.

He was a government spy! Shoes in fecal matter!

Something stinks in the State of Arkansas. Damned Government can stir up anyone's neuroses; make anyone paranoid. Perhaps she would have thought about this earlier and alerted Lowmax, had she not been so enthralled by both Beasley's monster-like appearance and his wild brutality. Lester the Molester may be correct, she thought. That Panopticon is power: seeing without being seen is like being a god. Focusing on a different matter, she debated whether the Justice Department would bring criminal charges against Orbis Laboratories, or, even worse, whether they would target her. No, no, they have no proof! Heh, heh, heh. If not proof, they might have at least some evidence. But what if they only have circumstantial evidence? Will they still prosecute?

A chill of terror cut through her heart.

# Chapter 9 — Cash Flow Problem

On Monday afternoon, Dr. Bates and Phil O. Kerdes, the Controller, met again. "Sure, no problem. I'll file the claim for vandalism immediately," Phil agreed. As they talked about other problems, Ivon's eyes focused on a picture on the wall: "Look, Phil. Doesn't dad look strong here? And Sabino and Tom Stone are so young! And the woman…I wonder who she is?"

Phil sighed. "Sammy-Lee, she was your father's research assistant, whom he recruited from Rutgers University. Never knew her too well, but I've heard Tom say that she was a brilliant scientist."

"So, Phil, how is the bottom line?"

Pleased that young Dr. Bates was taking an interest in the company, he continued, "I'm glad you'll be meeting with Alex. You know, sales are up and he's been shooting his mouth about how the entire company depends on him." As if agitated, Phil stood up. "Alex is a hard person, or, if you pardon the expression, a real pain in the ass. Your father hated his guts, but he put up with him because the guy is a master salesperson. And since his sales soared last year, making the bottom-line soar, he started making demands to your dad about ownership in the company. In fact, he already acts as if he were the President! Just don't let him walk all over you, Ivon—that domineering bastard."

Gazing at Phil, Dr. Bates wondered what his Controller was thinking. Whether Phil saw in him a scared, green young man, a scientist, a bookworm, an egghead—totally different from the old man. Joe Bates was a hyena who not only tore his enemies to shreds, but also ate them alive. But look at this pathetic young pup who never even says a bad word, let alone hurt anyone. As the pressure grows, the pup will haul ass on out of here. Dr. Bates pulled the threatening note he had found under his door and handed it to Phil. "What do you think?"

"A death threat…this is serious, Ivon!" Phil exclaimed as he rose to his feet. "Let's turn it over to Detective Wilkins. He'll have it analyzed for prints…"

"I agree. Now I'm getting scared."

"I heard from several reps in Marketing that Alex is threatening that if you don't appoint him President, he'll take his best customers with him and walk over to Orbis Laboratories, of all places."

"Helen McCain's company?" asked Ivon. "Is Alex serious?"

"He may be. A couple of weeks ago I saw him at the Circo having lunch and schmoozing with Henry Cook. You know Henry is McCain's top V.P. and henchman at Orbis Labs. He has a reputation as a real Don Juan and man about town, and people at Orbis call him Henry the Eight."

"Helen McCain again!" exclaimed Ivon, not because he was merely curious about her, but because an ill sensation stirred within him every time someone mentioned her name.

"Sabino just warned me about her, which makes me wonder if father and Helen McCain had a fling? I've heard that after mother died…"

"I've heard some rumors about that, too, but that was before my time," interrupted Phil. "I've also heard that your father spurned Helen after she lost a breast to cancer, but that was long before my time. You might know her chief of security disappeared a week after they killed your father. No one has ever heard a word about him. Nothing ever again. Detective Wilkins thinks this man—this Rashkin—killed your father, got his blood money, and then left the country."

"At times like these, I wish I could divine things," said Ivon. "Maybe this Rashkin is the killer. God knows every act and event…if we could just tap into that infinite intelligence…"

Phil returned to the subject. "I hear from people in the trade that McCain has beefed up her security forces. She's hired a former Secret Service guy, Lester Lowmax, as the new Chief of Security. This guy could be worse, meaner, more dangerous than Rashkin."

"Do you know what Alex wants?"

Phil nodded. "He wants more money, some ownership in the company, but more than that, he wants your job, Ivon. He wants to be President of Bates Pharmaceuticals! He's hungry for power. Detective Wilkins has been checking him out, too, and he thinks Alex had a lot to gain from your father's death. 'Motive' he called it."

Detecting a certain nervousness in Phil's voice, he let him talk.

"I sense something evil is going down. Just my gut reaction."

Phil removed his thick glasses and started polishing them with brisk, jerky movements.

"I feel the same way," agreed Ivon. "Like there's a storm brewing ahead. Anyway, did my father mention what Helen McCain's complaints were?"

"They just hated each other. And when Orbis lost the patent protection on several antibiotics—their best sellers, really, which were the company's cash cow—and we hit the market with generics, McCain blew her top and threatened to buy us out one day."

"Still, Orbis has grown at a rapid pace."

"Questionable takeovers mainly. Olin merging with E. R. Squibb, and then Squibb with Bristol-Myers, were legitimate, but Orbis's mergers are smelly. She's notorious for bust-up leveraged buyouts."

"Let's keep our eyes open. She may still want to buy us out."

"Yes, Ivon. That woman is evil, a woman of gutsy deeds but of low morals. Your father always said that she was in the throes of criminal insanity."

"Criminal insanity? Did father really say that?"

Ketty's officious voice crackled over the intercom, "A Miss Laura Standish on line 92, Ivon, and Detective Avery Wilkins is here."

Ambling over to his desk, he picked up the receiver. "Take Laura's number. I'll get back to her after I speak with detective Wilkins—offer my apologies. Show Mr. Wilkins in."

Ivon asked Phil, "tell me something before we talk to Detective Wilkins. I want to look ahead, and for my peace of mind, would you think an additional 5 million dollars in working capital might solve the cash flow problems?"

"That'll do it, Ivon. As the company grows, so must the cash grow."

"I think I can get a 5-million-dollar loan with another bank, a bank where a fraternity brother is a V. P. And since we have sixty days with Liberty, go ahead and order the research equipment Annie Norris and I need. I gave you the specifications."

"Why don't we order the equipment after you get the loan?"

"You go ahead and get the equipment," responded Ivon in a firm voice. "I'll find the money somehow, Phil. A research lab must have state-of-the-art equipment." He kept quiet, but he couldn't help thinking: If it were up to Phil and dad, they'd still be cutting the grass with machetes! Cheapskates. Ivon felt ambivalent about Phil, whom he saw as a deeply intelligent and loyal executive but a timid one. Didn't father often refer to Phil as "The company genius"?

But he recalled Sabino's words: "Phil is soft. You may have to step in and kick some ass with them bankers." Then his mind turned to Laura Standish: Ah, such a good looker! A long-legged beauty whose mere voice and image made his whole-body tingle with a thrill of pleasure.

Having liked detective Wilkins from the very first moment, Dr. Bates welcomed him with a vigorous, friendly handshake. He wore a charcoal-gray suit with a buttoned-down shirt and a solid silk tie. And as he looked into his eyes, he could still recall his soft, compassionate voice on the telephone: Blunt instrument. Maybe a heavy wrench…deep indentations…instant death. "Not your typical smart-alecky NYC cop one sees on TV shows," Dr. Bates thought.

"The commander wants some loose ends tied, so are there any other shareholders besides you and Ms. Van Osburgh?" asked Wilkins, wasting no time.

"No, the old man was a control freak," replied Ivon. "This has to be cross-referenced, bear with me please."

Dr. Bates saw him go back and forth between tabs, writing entries in the three-ring binder. Wilkins continued, "Did any executives have contracts with golden parachutes or stock option clauses?"

"Well, yes," Phil hastened to reply, "Alex Panagora has a contract and no one else. It's in the safe. I'll ask Ketty to make a copy. By the way, last week Alex was furious because he learned somebody had run a credit check on him and also looked into his bank accounts."

"Oh, yes," replied Detective Wilkins, and he grinned. "We aren't leaving any stones unturned. Even the IRS let us peek into the tax returns for some suspects on our short list. So far, I've found no shocking revelations in the tax forms and bank accounts. Everybody's clean, including you, Mr. Kerdes. That Peter Rashkin, Orbis's former Chief of Security, is missing…perhaps fled the country, has lifted some of the pressure; still, I ran a check with

Interpol and found nothing. The commander wants me to wrap up the case. But I'm not quite satisfied."

Dr. Bates handed him the note.

Detective Wilkins said, "Let me run this through the Latent Fingerprint Unit. The killer or killers may still be loose out there, someone you all know and trust, because your father's killer was no professional killer for sure. I still think the criminal was someone he trusted enough to turn his back on…since they bludgeoned him from behind."

Phil suggested, "Could you arrange for an undercover agent to protect Dr. Bates? That's a serious threat and right in his apartment, no less."

"I'll ask the Chief. But I wouldn't count on it. I recommend you get a private guard, someone big and burly, whose mere presence would act as a deterrent."

And just as softly as he had come in, the good detective padded out. Dr. Bates felt that nothing had escaped the eyes of the good detective. You can tell he was soaking up every little detail. Yes sir, the way he drawled about contracts and stock options. Did he pay close attention to hands and eyes? You bet, as if he was expecting to detect tremors and fever, there he was picking up every dissonant tone. Moreover, some strange quality or other set Detective Wilkins apart from his peers.

Pondering about that strange quality, Laura Standish came to his mind. Oh, yes, must hasten to get a date with her. She is brilliant, connected—an heiress who could be of so much help in the future. Laura, Lor, Lo, luscious, lusty, lovely! Longing for her, he pictured her running through grassy malls and green meadows, blending with thickets and shrubs, her diaphanous robe fluttering and yielding a length of thigh, her hair streaming in the wind. And as she turned, he glimpsed a virginal smile, chaste and pure. His heart speeded and a sweet thrill of bliss gagged him. She is a sweet goddess indeed, one who gives both so much hope and yet so much fear. But what if she says no? Only after he considered this possibility did his bliss end, prompting him to ask himself, "Will Cecilia ever accept Laura?"

# Chapter 10 — Cowboy learns the ropes

Having taken Joey De Lemos under his wing, Dr. Jeffrey Loomis—the Production Director of Bates Pharmaceuticals—enjoyed teaching him how to mix the raw materials, how to pipe the syrup to Bottling, and to do the required paperwork. Dr. Loomis was an intense and often curt person, but unusually calm and patient with Cowboy, who wondered if Tom Stone had—for some unknown reason—asked him to go easy on him.

"As soon as you complete each batch, call me. Pipe nothing next door to Bottling unless I've signed off on the job order. If you're sloppy, the main office will scream that they can't calculate the joint-product costs or the separable costs—whatever. And of course, you also have to deal with Pia Pecunia first, right here in the Plant. You'll get to know her soon enough, and believe me, she's a most unpleasant woman to deal with. Ugh, as soon as you learn the ropes, I want you to deal directly with her and good luck. The old serpent drives me nuts with that religious gibberish and mumble jumble, not to mention the loose undergarments she wears. Or shall we say tight undergarments?"

Pausing, as if disgusted by the mere mention of the name Pia, he continued, "Anyway, after you master the routines, I will get you started on Quality Control-QC. I'll teach you to operate the gas chromatograph and the mass spectrometer."

"Yo, man. That sounds so-o intense!"

Because Joey De Lemos took great care in his bearing, so that his blue uniform was always crisp and clean, the nametag over his right shirt pocket well-polished. He always appeared well groomed. By now, everyone in the Plant called him "Cowboy." In the second week, Dr. Loomis let him work on his own.

A full hour, cool! Cowboy thought.

He set out to find a place where he could smoke a little roach with nobody busting chops. The damned bottlers were all busy keeping up with the conveyor belts. He watched the operation: filling, capping, labeling, and boxing. What an infernal noisy department! Sauntering down toward the west wing, he turned to Shipping and Receiving where he hung around for some time talking to Felix and his workers.

Bored, Joey asked, "Is there a bathroom around here?"

Felix pointed to the far corner. Five minutes later Felix and his crew heard Sabino's dogs growling and snarling. Stopping what they were doing, the workers looked at each other for an instant before they took off to see what the problem was. Standing a foot from the large cage and holding a two-by-four in his right hand, Cowboy was taunting the dog, swiping the slat sideways on the vertical iron bars. After each swipe, he'd smack a vicious blow to the top of the cage.

Felix yelled, "What the hell are you doing, man? Don't mess with them dogs!"

"Stinking dogs started barking at me for no reason at all."

"What stinks is marijuana smoke," said Felix, sniffing around.

Putting the slat down, he swaggered away, legs slightly bowed, his cowboy boots—the metal half-moon heels—clicking loud on the hard floor.

* * * *

When Sabino went to feed Debates and Rebates, he saw the cage was a mess, the dogs' blankets soaking wet. The dogs seemed agitated, nervous, and instead of their normal growl, they yelped, moaned, and whimpered. Their almond-shaped eyes, deeply set, and their heads cocked to one side, seemed to point at something on the floor. Sabino's eyes darted to the point and saw the two-by-four lying there. He picked it up and rushed to Shipping and Receiving, where Felix told him the full story. Without wasting a second, Sabino headed towards Syrups. Kicking the metal doors open, he bolted for the far corner of the room where Cowboy was reading a chemistry manual and listening to a small radio tuned to a popular New York City station. Cowboy scrambled to his feet and stepped back, his back against the wall.

"What's your problem, man?"

With Cobra-like speed, Sabino thrust the two-by-four straight out like a lance into the young man's stomach just below the ribs, knocking the wind out of Cowboy. As Joey doubled up and fell to his knees, he tried to breathe, but his windpipe felt plugged on both ends. The old man raked the two-by-four over his throat and slowly lifted him up, the rough, splintered end of the slat scratching and pressing hard against his windpipe, choking him. Cowboy thought the old man was going to kill him by crushing his trachea.

"Mess with my dogs again and you will take your last breath." Cowboy stood semi-conscious against the wall. His face blanched.

"Keep your stick," Sabino hissed, and with a swift blow he crashed the slat on the small radio and the music stopped, shards of plastic and wire flying in all directions.

Sabino turned around and left.

For a moment, the young man's mind crowded with wicked vengeful notions, notions that made him want to turn evil. "No, no," he mumbled, and cleared the evil thoughts. "I can't blame this on the old man. No, of course not. Live and learn. That's some tough hombre! What people say about Sabino ain't just idle talk, he is fearless! Felix says he's fought Cubans, Colombians, even the mafia, and what about that talk about him wrestling and burning up a vampire. And not your regular vampire, but one of the undead! If Sabino wasn't afraid of Dracula's cousin, then he can't be afraid of anyone. A tough old man, that Sabino! Hard to believe for sure, but people talk an awful lot about that bloodsucker as if he really existed. Felix says Sabino actually fought two vampires, a father and a son. And that he killed the father, but he let the child go. Hmm, where there's smoke, there's fire, and where there's ashes, there must have been a fire." But then a weightier notion—an obsession, something he felt was missing in his life — came over him and he promised himself must not to lose sight of that.

The next day, at about four in the afternoon, Cowboy was hurrying along the Raw Materials area when he saw Jossie—Josephine Lott, the supervisor—standing by the door. Though heavy, Jossie had shapely legs and thin ankles that carried her with graceful steps.

"Hey Cowboy, what's new?" Jossie called. "I hear you've been messing around with some scrawny, puny, pencil-necked girl in Janos' department. I figured you for a man who likes his women fleshy, healthy, in full bloom."

"You got it, Jossie. The fuller the better."

"Don't wait too long, or it might be too late. You know Angelo, the UPS guy, the body builder…he's been dying to get some of this." Slapping loudly the flanks of her abundant buttocks, she cocked a hip and smiled.

"Gotta run, I gotta clean my vats…I'm going to have sweet dreams tonight, Jossie. I'm gonna dream of Beauty and the Beast. I'm going to dream that you're the beauty and I am the beast."

"You, big tease, calling me a beauty."

"A beauty…and also the best!" Between his teeth: "That's a lot of woman! Every woman is a beauty in her own way."

Gazing after him, Jossie then turned to the group that had gathered by her desk: "Wow, I wanna get me some of that! Hmmm…suck that curling lip, yank that ponytail and…wrap them bowed legs around my waist."

Behind Jossie's back, Imani, after winking at Toni and elbowing Crystal, said, "Keep dreaming." Tony Lisanti, an assistant warehouse manager, said, "You have lots of competition, Jossie. Luz tells me Melissa La Monalisa's got the hots for that boy too, and you know La Monalisa can really strut her charms with those miniskirts that look more like hot pants than skirts."

"Melissa's locked in," replied Jossie. "Nobody can go in that office because of the freezer with the controlled substances. There's no way Joey can go there. Besides, he'd have to go through Pia first, and you know Pia Pecunia can be the biggest pain in the ass—the old bat!"

The group was so engrossed in their chit-chat that they hadn't noticed the Warehouse Manager, Miss Meneses, standing by the entrance and glaring at them. Before the solemn Miss Meneses even cleared her throat, the group scattered as if they had seen a ghost.

At about four-thirty, Cowboy was wrapping up for the day when Connie, Janos' assistant, sidled into his corral. No sooner did he see her than he dashed to the door, pulling her in gently. She was a swan-necked young woman, gorgeous strands and tendrils of auburn hair curling on that graceful neck.

"Janos sent me to Tom's office to deliver the paperwork." Her tender voice set Cowboy aflame.

"Connie, babe. Come in for a couple of minutes…a few little minutes, that's all."

She stepped in. "Okay, Joey, but promise, not a second longer!" And indeed, without wasting a second, Cowboy steered her to the side of the huge wooden vat near the entrance. The vat was an old wooden model that sat on metal legs—to prevent moisture and corrosion—leaving a space between the elevated vat and the tiled floor of about two feet.

Holding hands, giggling, and kissing, they slid under the vat. The tightness of the spot and their own daring whipped them up into a frenzy of passion. It's so damp and musty, man.

"I can't breathe," Connie moaned. "It's too tight."

After a few moments of torrid love making, they both got overheated and breathless. A little rest won't hurt anybody…catch our breaths.

"Cowboy," Connie whispered, still panting, "I've got to get back."

"One more time, you gorgeous babe…"

Unwilling to remain any longer, Connie protested when they heard the door opening, creaking slowly. What's that? They heard the din from the corridor, the ebb and flow of nervous workers getting ready to wrap up, to wash up, to go home. As the noise got louder, the door smacked wide open.

"Come on in, let me fix you a drink," they heard a voice say.

Cowboy rolled off Connie quietly, wriggling sideways, stretching his neck towards the light. Ah, Dr. Loomis! Look at those old shoes. You can see the bulging toes tweaking to go through the soft leather. Cowboy whispered, "It's Doctor Loomis."

Connie kept quiet.

As Dr. Loomis and Janos ambled toward the desk, Cowboy could hear Dr. Loomis drop his clipboard on the desk.

"How's the gutsy blond kid doing?"

Cowboy felt Connie's muscles stiffen taut. Aha! Connie's recognized Janos' voice. Bad move keeping her this long, but too late now, dude. "The guy is too wild."

"He is crazy, if you ask me. I'm glad he ain't in my section; seems like he'd be a tough kid to control."

"But a quick learner, and he's sharp as a tack. In the twenty years I've been here, I've never seen a worker so crazy about the Plant, and I'd say he even cares for this place more than both Sabino and old Joe Bates together. I wonder where he gets that attitude? You don't find workers like him anymore, a tough kid, but with a wonderful attitude towards work. He does more work than ten men put together."

Tickling Connie playfully, as if happy with the compliments, he made Connie shrink back, the ring of keys dropping out of her pocket. Since the skirt of her uniform was riding high—all hiked up over her waist, the keys made a distinctive metallic noise as they hit the tiled floor.

"What's that?" Janos asked with alarm in his voice.

"The damn pipes in the vats," explained Dr. Loomis, "they contract as they cool off and start making noises. Here, cheers!"

"Damned keys are making me paranoid," complained Janos. "I swear I just heard my own keys clinking under that vat. Let me look around."

Getting down on his knees, Janos looked behind a gleaming cylinder of liquefied nitrogen. But just then Dr. Loomis patted him on the shoulder and said, "C'mon, drink up! You can stay here and look until next week if you want to, but I'm going home."

Janos scowled. "I got to get home, too. I wonder where that little bitch Connie is? I sent her on an errand and gave her my keys to get back in the lab. Now I don't know where she is."

"I saw a bunch of girls lollygagging by Jossie's."

Dr. Loomis and Janos pushed the doors open and went out.

With fear in her eyes and lust in his, Connie and Cowboy slithered out from under the vat. She tried to say something but couldn't utter a sound, feeling paralyzed. So silent was the hallway that when the wall-telephone right behind her rang out with a loud, long ring, she jumped a foot off the floor, tears coursing down her pale face as she tore out of there like a greyhound on a fast break, Cowboy gazing after her, observing the spattering of debris sticking to the large sweat-wet spot on her back.

Cowboy answered the phone. "Okay Melissa, babe, I'll pick you up at six-thirty. Later."

Feeling remorseful about causing a problem for Connie, he trudged to his desk, opened the left bottom drawer, and gently laid Connie's panties there. Then he ambled to the first glimmering stainless-steel vat, and spreading his arms wide, he hugged it. Next, he moved to the other vats and did the same thing, and when he hugged the wooden vat he whispered, "I love you, you old timer — senior citizen." He strode to the wall—a blood-red brick wall similar to the building's outer walls—where the telephone was anchored. Stretching his arms wide open, he leaned his face against the wall, feeling the rough texture of the bricks scraping against the incipient stubble on his face, exclaiming,

"I love you bricks. I love you wall. I love you Plant!"

He remembered his mom bringing him to the Plant when he was a child, many times in fact. With his arms still extended, he pledged, "I will lay my life on the line for this old Plant. Now, if Tom, Sabino, or Dr. Bates ever need me for anything dangerous, I will be there, and I will never say no, regardless of personal sacrifice. All my life I've longed to work here at Bates, just like my mom did. I feel I belong here, that this is my Plant, a building that's in my blood."

Overwhelmed by emotion, a strong emotion that made him giddy and faint, he felt the room swirling and his body floating. And then, dropping to his knees, he saw the vats spin and orbit around his head faster and faster, and he felt his knees yield as he collapsed in a heap. Attacks of lightheadedness had been hitting him more often lately, and he didn't know why. After a short while, by clawing on the wall, he got back on his feet and there he stood on rickety legs for a moment. Ever since the Gulf War! Is it Gulf Syndrome illness? Scared and confused by the severity of the attack, he prayed:

"God, please don't let me be ill! Maybe that damned Colombian weed is baking my brains. Help me, dear Lord, and I promise I'll cut back."

Feeling that the numbness in his legs had faded, and that his mind was now clear, he left to meet Melissa La Monalisa.

They had dinner at the Valencia Restaurant, a Cuban restaurant in Union City famous for its Cuban delicacies. Cowboy told Melissa he had to leave early because he had promised his elderly neighbors he would do some grocery shopping for them. "They're old folks I've known all my life. Mr. D'Agostino's about ninety now, and his wife is eighty-six, I think."

"May I tag along, Joey?" "Of course, let's go."

He shopped at the Grand Union Supermarket in Ridgefield Park. A few minutes before nine, he rang the bell and in a second, Mrs. D'Agostino opened the door.

"This is my friend, Melissa," said Cowboy, as they marched into the kitchen and deposited the three brown bags there.

"Oh, my," Mrs. D'Agostino said, "I don't know what I'd do without you." Cowboy rose and disappeared down the hallway.

"He's checking the house,"

Mrs. D'Agostino whispered. "He always does that, ever since Leo got messed up in the head. He's so useless now. Alzheimer's! My poor dear, he barely recognizes me sometimes. And me, too. Losing my memory."

"Don't you have any family, Mrs. D'Agostino?" asked Melissa.

"My granddaughter, Terry. She and Joey grew up together, and she now lives in Edison, Exit Thirteen…or is it Exit Eighteen? But she can't visit us because she has leukemia and is undergoing chemotherapy treatment."

"How awful, Mrs. D'Agostino," said Melissa. "Leukemia is cancer of the blood; I had a friend—*fwen*—who passed away from that. Is Terry's—came out *tegwees*—condition fatal?"

"I'm afraid so."

"So sorry." So *sowee* "Joey will keep an eye on you."

"Oh, yes. This young man's heart is in the right place. This Alzheimer's thing is such a cruel thing because it robs human beings of their dignity. Leo was a great athlete, he was a swimmer, and he made the Olympic team in 1922. Look at my poor dear now! And I could recite *Romeo and Juliet* by heart."

When Cowboy returned, he hugged and bid good night to Mrs. D'Agostino, whose eyes suddenly looked teary and almost panicky. By the front door, the old lady grabbed Melissa's hand—a terrified stare now glowing in her eyes—not letting Melissa's hand go, "Tell me my dear—what is this young man's name?"

Repressing a sigh of compassion, Melissa whispered, "Joey. He will always look out for you, so, don't be afraid."

"Ah, Lee's boy, yes of course—Sammy Lee's boy! She used to work at Bates, you know." she exclaimed, her eyes now placid as if immersed in a nostalgic past. "When did he get so tall; my, how time passes. You're from Jersey— right?"

"Weehawken, Mrs. D'Agostino, on the river." *On-negweeveh.* "By the Lincoln Tunnel. It's so noisy you can hear the cars screeching—*scweeching*—all night long, but the view is lovely, you can even see the Twin Towers from my house."

# Chapter 11 — Wooing Laura

At about 6 p.m. Victor drove Ivon to the Brooke, Sterne and Benz building on Park Avenue near Grand Central Station, where Ivon released Victor for the day. Ivon had hoped to see Laura by herself, but she and three coworkers were standing by the corner door, chatting and laughing. When he approached them, they fell silent, but Laura—with exquisite grace—introduced Ivon to the group.

Ivon asked, “Laura and I haven’t made any plans. Why don’t you join us for a few cocktails? My treat.”

“Excellent idea, Ivon,” Laura said. “Let’s go to Le Bistroquet on East 54th; they make terrific Margaritas, Martinis, and Bloody Mary’s.” An older woman in the group excused herself, since she had tickets for the Nets game at Madison Square Garden. The other two younger women agreed to come along. Stephanie, a broker trainee, said, “One drink is my limit, two will give me a headache for three days.” Cristina, a senior stock analyst, was enthusiastic. “I’ve heard of Le Bistroquet, I’ll go, but I must leave by seven.”

When they got there, Ivon took in the scene: not bad, Le Bistroquet, a hangout for the young crowd. Stephanie keeps that well-shaped mouth busy. Off-color jokes…fine delivery though. Right after she left, Cristina couldn’t resist a jab. “No doubt Stephanie will make a terrific saleswoman. I’ve never seen a rapper with such a long rap, a rap that wraps around an entire city block.” Two drinks later, Cristina also left. After a fine dinner at Charlotte’s on West 52nd Street, Laura and Ivon hailed a cab and went to Stringfellows on East 21st. Laura loved to dance and Ivon obliged, but after a couple of sets, he pointed to his knees and said, “Sorry, my knees…” Since the crowd at the bar was thick, they moved to the balcony where it was quieter; Laura drank margaritas and Ivon beer.

Seeing Ivon cross his long legs and rubbing his right knee, Laura said, “I saw you play a few times, a few Ivy League games. The basketball groupies revered you.”

“Those were fun years,” said Ivon with a nostalgic tone in his voice.

Laura sipped her drink. “But now, how does it feel to run a good-sized company, Ivon?”

"We also need to automate and buy some expensive research equipment." "You'll need capital."

"Very much so."

"When you're ready, you let me know. I'd love to take your company public; I have lots of experience now and great connections for an Initial Public Offering—IPO for Bates stock. Look at my track record; just last year I took a Biochem firm public. The IPO price was $4.30 and adjusting for splits they're now worth $139."

"Wow! That's incredible."

Please help me capitalize Bates Pharmaceuticals." Laura said. "Of course, that's my expertise. Let Irene go ahead with some

articles she has in mind, to pave the way…investors are always on the look-out for new promising faces and you are a promising face. Irene's articles in the Journal will help, but you need to engage a PR agency. Believe me, these public relations people are image experts and you need to spread goodwill about the company."

Dr. Bates stared at her. A career woman—an investment banker and lawyer—with exceptional skills in corporate finance…she's all business. This is someone who can help the company. Cecilia's got it wrong. She isn't a conniving gold-digger, but an ambitious young woman. That's all. And what is wrong with a young woman having ambition? Cecilia overreacted and took a dislike to her because she is being overprotective.

"Of course, I want you to," Ivon smiled. "You do not know how happy I am I ran into you." He remembered how he had met her for the first time, right in front of Marquand Chapel, and later how he had heard the frat boys refer to her as The Wharton princess who lives in The House of Mirth and who sails with IRS friends. At that time, the allusion had meant to him she was an heir to the Wharton family, or perhaps that she was bound for the Wharton School of Business in Philadelphia.

"Maybe I should pay you a retainer for your advice."

"No need. If the deal comes through, my company makes a lot of money and, of course, I'll get a fat bonus. When we are ready, my company will prepare a standard contract. Let me tell you something, Ivon. I feel it in my bones that when Bates Pharmaceuticals' stock hits the Street, it will be an immediate hot issue. Now if you have glamorous new products—that's it! The market price of the shares would soar to unbelievable heights. Bates Pharmaceuticals could well be the Johnson & Johnson of tomorrow!"

Staring at her for a moment to catch her attention, he said: "Look straight toward the mirror behind the bar." Laura stuck her delicate chin out and looked straight ahead, her eyes sparkling with curiosity. Ivon kept quiet, and Laura was now puzzled. "You have the most beautiful profile I've ever seen in a woman," says he.

Neither poise nor wit helped her to come up with a quick riposte. Lowering her lovely violet eyes in utter embarrassment, she said, "Oh, Ivon, I will never fall for that again—you set me up! I bet you say that to all the girls…"

Ivon clasped Laura's slender hand. "Slow dance?"

As they headed to the dance floor, Ivon turned to the bar and his eyes locked with the eyes of a hulking man who smiled a crooked smile. The hairs on his neck stood on end. Who the devil is this man?

He held Laura close, and he felt her breasts and her flat abdomen against his body. She squirmed and pulled back. Slow down—he chided himself—don't rush things. She'll come around. Timing's important here, don't blow it with that sophomoric rush. Gazing into her eyes, her high cheekbones, and generous mouth, he could hardly restrain himself from squeezing her and kissing her. Running his hand over her silky hair, he smelled the fragrance of an herbal shampoo. When he clasped his large hand around her small waist, his heart raced so fast that he had to take shallow breaths of air, air that he let out in quiet puffs.

If not a goddess, at least a princess indeed!

Feeling a deep spasm and an animalistic craving, he realized how alone he had been after he had parted with Cassandra. Cassandra is the past; Laura is the here and now.

A sensation of danger chilled his spine. As they returned to the table, Ivon saw the hulking man again. Yes, the same man standing in the shadows, a silhouette with a protruding paunch. A form that reminded him of Degas' oil Dancers, Pink and Green, except this man had no hat. He had first seen the same man at Barnes & Noble, later at Columbus Circle, talking to the mounted police, and now here.

This same man! Realizing the man was stalking him, he felt nauseous. Never had he felt raw flight fear, fear for his own life and also for Laura's. He all but grabbed Laura by the arm to flee, but he bridled the terror that had seized his senses. Anger first, and then rage filled his heart. God knows what this man is up to, yet a man has to take a stand and behave like a man. But how to do that if the man is a coward? Sabino's words echoed in his mind: An upright man is a man that fears God, defends his women, and honors them with nobility—God and honor, Ivon; or what is man for?

When he saw the bulking shadow bound toward the restroom, the music stopped. Sabino's words goaded him to do something—less from the thought that he was a coward, than from the fear that the man could hurt Laura. Something that he could not allow to happen. He held his breath, and with a phantom voice, he said,

"I'll be back in a minute, Laura."

Pushing the men's room door open, he saw the large man drying his hands with a paper towel, and two other men were at the urinals. Standing in the center of the room, he stared at the hulk-man.

"Why are you following me?" he asked in a low monotone, his heart racing. Taken aback for a second, the man recovered only to ignore him, heading for the door. Ivon stepped in to block the way.

"Who's paying you…what do you want with me?"

As the man tried to skirt to the left, Ivon shoved him against the urinals; the other two men moved out of the way. "If you have a problem with me, that's okay. Come after me—I can take care of myself. But if any harm comes to that girl, you'll be sorry. Who's paying you?"

They stared at each other, two big men facing each other in deep silence. The hulk-man yielded,

"Nobody—you're mistaken."

Ivon saw the man smile, a crooked smile that showed crooked teeth, and as he moved in closer, he yelled in the man's face,

"If I see you again following me, I'll kick your fat ass…"

As if to make room to throw a punch, the hulk-man bumped his chest against Ivon, a hostile move that caused Ivon to bend his knees and yank the man down with a two-leg pull down. Whomp!

They both landed hard on the floor, with Ivon finding his balance, twisting the man's arm behind his back and making him groan. As the man rolled over to loosen the grip, Ivon caught a glint of cold, deadly blueness snug in a leather shoulder holster. A gun! When Ivon attempted to go for the gun—Thunk!—he felt a thick thud behind his ear followed by a bolt of lightning crackling and firing up an expanding universe of bright variegated lights.

Only after two minutes did he blink his eyes. Dr. Bates saw two nervous men holding wet paper towels against his brow while others were gazing down at him.

"What happened?" he asked in a raspy voice.

A thin young man wearing an expensive business suit said, "This bald-headed ape with no eyebrows came behind you and hit you with a stick, just when you had the other goon ready to cry uncle—looks like the hit you with a cop's club or something. That was some whack, man! These two gorillas must be gangsters…they both had guns!"

Ivon returned to the table, "What took you so long?" Laura teased.

After staring at the two young guys that were hovering around Laura, trying to hit on her; and though he felt weak and sore, he snarled at them,

"Hey, you two—take a hike!"

Not a second did the pair waste in melding into the crowd. Turning to Laura, he said, "Let's get out of here. A goon hit me in the head and knocked me out and may have scrambled my brains. I need to see a doctor right away!"

# Chapter 12 — The Interview

Stuart Potter—a fraternity brother and a senior V.P. at Manufacturers Hanover Trust—agreed to consider a 5-million dollar; he also wished to assume the loan that Bates had with Liberty National Bank. “We have to hang on and survive for a few weeks,” Ivon murmured, worried. “This influx of cash from Manufacturers will make our controller happy and he’ll stop going around grinding his teeth, complaining how that lab equipment is going to drain the cash flow. A good man, Phil Kerdes is, but a cautious good man! He plays it much too safe to be sure. Are all accountants like that?” Ketty’s voice came on the intercom, “Irene Cohen, from the Wall Street Journal, will be here in twenty minutes.”

“Oh, yes,” Ivon whispered to himself. A warm feeling went through him as he pictured her: cute despite that Peter Pan haircut, an androgynous person—to be sure. But that feeling yielded to a jolt of icy fear: Detective Wilkins’s had told him he had placed an undercover man to watch the office. Such a creepy feeling! Who’d be so evil as to resort to threats, to violence? Laura Standish’s image popped into his mind and that made him feel better, but not for long, for doubts and ill thoughts overcame him. Might Laura be one of these ambitious, pushy, career-oriented women? Cecilia is right in distrusting her, thinking she’s a plotting woman. If one could only see what is in people’s hearts! Now his heart pounded, and he was unsure whether it was from fear of death or fear that Laura might reject him. After all, she is an independent professional young woman who could have her pick of the City’s most eligible young men of the IRS—the Immensely Rich Set. “Build an image for Bates Pharmaceuticals,” Laura Standish had urged him. “Let Irene Cohen interview you. Let her write a favorable article for the Journal.” He pondered about their friendship: “I guess they are good friends, as Brian—old brain-dead, ‘Beedee’—Dedrick and I are good close friends. Well, today, Wednesday, Irene is starting the interviews about Bates Pharmaceuticals and there’s no reason to be nervous. Let’s go along with the gag.”

So cheerful was Irene that he no longer felt as depressed as a moment ago.

"How far back do you want me to go?"

"Genesis, Ivon, in the beginning…from the top. First, when was the company founded, and where and how?"

"My father, Joseph Bates, went to work for his uncle Carter Bates after he left the army. Uncle Carter made pesticides. One day, a bum shot and killed uncle Carter in plain daylight. Dad took over the business."

"Was your father accused?"

"No, no, several witnesses knew and saw the killer and the police caught him. Dad had saved his Vietnam combat pay and with that money, he kept the company going. The lab was in an old building on Tenth Avenue and 33rd Street in Manhattan; an area infested with bums, winos, and many criminals. Dad tracked down Sabino—an old faithful and tough Army buddy—and hired him. He tasked him to rid the area of all the derelicts. Sabino did that and people weren't afraid to work in that building anymore. By 1970, the company had ten employees. Sabino and Dad built the company to the size it is now; of course, with some capital from a lady friend he had."

So vivid and melancholy were the remembrances that he felt to be reliving the experiences and conversations—which were lifelike hallucinations—he'd had as a child with the workers, but in particular with Sabino.

"So, the next step was the move to New Jersey?" Irene asked.

—New Jersey? asked little Ivon, why did father move the company to New Jersey, Sabino? Couldn't he find another Plant in Manhattan?

—Because your father had a vision, Ivon, replied Sabino, and with animation, he started talking to little Ivon as if he was talking to an adult. Your father knew soon we would need a lot of space, water, sewers, electricity, roads, and land. New Jersey had all that, plus the marshes. Also, many pharmaceutical suppliers had moved there. You could smell the chemicals from the Turnpike.

"Yes, Irene, that was the next step," Dr. Bates answered and repeated, "it was the next step and a bold step, too. They rented three U-Haul trucks and in one trip, they moved everything. July 6th, 1970, that's when they moved. That day my father locked the old building on 33rd Street, never to return to it."

The child had heard the story many times, but he never tired of it. He demanded:

—Tell me about the first day in the new Plant, Sabino.

—We had three rented trucks in the convoy, crossed the George Washington Bridge, and as we rode through several small towns we got lost. We took the wrong turn and soon we were driving through a cemetery!

Irene said, "July is always bright and shiny; a fine day for a bold move. Your father had some guts to take such a big step. A bold and scary move."

—Were you scared, Sabino? asked the child.

Little Ivon's eyes opened wide with fear every time Sabino mentioned the cemetery.

—I've never visited a cemetery, the child continued. Father doesn't even want to take me to the cemetery where mother rests. And Cecilia and Antonia always shut up every time I mention her. Anyway, did you get out of the cemetery right away?

—Nope, answered Sabino with some relish, teasing the child, taking a long pause. Your father, who led the convoy, stopped his car and signaled the caravan to stop. He gathered the men in a semicircle and, facing the cemetery, he asked us to pray with him. Well, your dad bowed his head and exclaimed,

> 'Dear Lord, author of us all, forgive our sins, for no one is pure but you. We shall work and prosper free from all evil and we will do it the American way: we will manufacture fair products in our new Plant.'

Irene: "Did your father take you to the Plant when you were a child?"

"Often," replied Ivon and his eyes shone with a felt pain for the countless times that his father had turned him over to Sabino and Felix in Shipping and Receiving, disappearing for the rest of the day. "Sabino, one of the old-timers, a founder and pioneer who still works at the plant, is like a second father to me. I told you earlier, he and father served together in Vietnam; they were POWs for a few days and escaped together thanks to a Filipino soldier and his dog. Sabino and the dog saved Dad's life, dragging him through rice paddies to safety."

Irene said, "Moving the factory and feeling responsible for the employees must have made your father nervous. It's fascinating to learn how an enterprise grows, to see the energy that moves it forward. What happened after they prayed?"

—The sun blazed with a light so bright the men had to shield their eyes with both hands over their brows, said Sabino, taking on a mocking poetic tone. I swear I saw a tiny star cross the sky and land in the swamp. As the men looked up into the cloudless blue sky, they saw a flock of geese flying southwest in glorious V-formation.

'Is that a sign, or what? It's an omen…they are pointing the way for us!' Rufus Redcoles shouted.

—Did you smell the stink from the swamp right away, Sabino?

—Oh, yeah. It's a small swamp though, more like a marsh. The smell ain't that bad on account of the Hackensack River, which flows under and brings up freshwater. There's a whirlpool in the center of the marsh, a wonderful, spooky swamp. The building was spooky, too, all them towers, heavy walls, stained glass…a mix between a church and a castle. Spooky yet inviting, quiet and deafening, and in word: scary.

—Who went inside the building first?

—Nobody. The bats and vampires hanging halfway to the floor from the high beams like droopy black flags scared us. Lots of them, many of them…squadrons, battalions, wings…made your skin crawl.

—Aw, Sabino. Stop pulling my leg! Protested the child. Bats and vampires are small, they don't grow to the size of flags. You have a way of stretching the truth, and I don't like that. You spoil the story…you're always doing that, like Sancho Panza."

—We all stayed outside for a while till your father walked to the front iron gates and opened them.

—Who shook the beehive? Asked little Ivon.

—I don't know, said Sabino shrugging his shoulders, I only know that we all ran to the gates. Them bees sounded like a squadron of airplanes! They stung 'Wagging-ass' Rufus Redcoles in the butt, eyebrow, neck, and hands.

Pulling and folding up the eyelid of his bad eye and exposing a full veiny eye-ball, Sabino twisted his neck sideways, stiffened his hands like grotesque claws, and walked around with clumsy steps mimicking a monster. He grunted:

—Pongo, pongo, attchuuu, attchuuu…gotcha, gotcha! atchupongo, atch- upongo, I have got you!

—You are silly, Sabino, that monster doesn't scare me.

—For many months we taunted poor Rufus about that sting, continued Sabino out of his monster role. The guys said it served him right because of his oversized lard ass. Old Rufus was the oldest worker and fat and, of course, he couldn't run as fast as the rest of us.

—When you were inside, what did you do first?

—We moved slow," Sabino explained, the old plant had everything Bates Druggists, Inc., needed. It took us a few weeks to adjust to the extra space. Them enormous bays, flying ceilings, cave-like dusty naves, grand halls, and long empty abandoned basements gave you the creeps! And yet like a church: all the spaces boomed with the least noise; we even had to lower our voices to avoid echoes. Rufus Redcoles, a good-natured man with a fair falsetto imitation of the Platters' Only You, farted so loud that scared them vampires away toward the swamp. Sabino would tease the boy, knowing the child's prim manners and knowing that Cecilia and Antonia would never allow little Ivon to utter vulgar words. He did it to teach to boy the realities of a vulgar world.

—That's a bad word, Sabino! Mom doesn't want me to say bad words. She says, 'lower functions of the body,' covers all that. But you enjoy saying nasty things. She says God made the body in his image and it is a temple. It's not funny! You are so gross.

—Ain't nothing gross or wrong talking about the human body! I am not a learned man, but I've heard that a wise man, a poet I think, once said: Love is a fart of the heart.

—Stop that! Quit it, Sabino. Now tell me, is it true what people say that you burned a vampire alive? People say you tortured him till he talked and told you his name. I don't believe it!

Irene's eyes shined with an eagerness to learn more facts: "So the first name of the company was Bates Druggists? I guess your father changed the name because the term 'druggist' picked up a bad ring."

—What happened to Rufus Redcoles, Sabino?"

—He was the first one of the original ten to die. But Natalie Redcoles, his daughter, is with us. She works in Household

Products.

—I know her, the child said with an impish look, and since I'm hungry, I'm going to see her right now. I hope she brought those juicy chicken wings for lunch. Mmm, yummy for my tummy.

"Is it time for lunch, Ivon?" asked Irene and she uncrossed her legs. She was a small red-haired young woman, with visible freckles on her face, and mannerisms that were neither feminine nor masculine. "I can't believe how time flies. I can't wait until you tell me about the attempts on your father's life. And I am also intrigued about Sabino burning a vampire alive, a vampire that has a name no less. We have a mystery here! No doubt you have a logical explanation for that; I can't wait to hear it."

"Well, Sabino never talked about that in detail. Only once I remember him talking about that and teasing me and trying to scare me by telling me the vampire had a name."

Irene's eyes glittered with confusion, but she kept quiet. Yet Ivon could tell that she wanted to find out the vampire was one of the regular biological species and not a crossover from the undead, a Dracula-like one.

Unable to restrain herself, she asked, "So, what's the name?"

"Sybellius."

"C'mon, Ivon! Sybellius is the name of a composer—you're pulling my leg."

"Let's go to lunch. How about some tuna sashimi, hand rolls, and clams? But leave the tape recorder behind; lunch will be off the record. I'll tell you who I think killed my father—someone who hates me and is trying to scare me. Even kill me, too."

With an impish smile, Irene said, "And I have some fiendish gossip to tell you about someone who doesn't hate you, nor is trying to scare you nor kill you, but is trying to help you. Wants to make your company grow larger than John & Johnson, Pfizer, and Procter all put together!"

# Chapter 13 — Jersey Assignment

Because the plant in Long Island City—which manufactured tablets, pills, capsules, and lozenges—was an important part of Orbis, Helen McCain threw a temper fit when she learned the plant had to close for a few days. Burglars, robbers, addicts, or bums vandalized the storage and warehouses, perhaps looking for controlled substances. Three times in a month! So, she put the heat on Lester Lowmax.

Lester the Molester had Lieutenant Edmond Wesley, the supervisor in charge, on the carpet. Wesley was arguing for the construction of a chain-link fence twelve-foot-high, set with concrete anchors and some razor ribbon on top.

Beasley and Morales walked in.

Lowmax said, "Listen up! Helen McCain feels the Bates people are working on a drug that will blow our good sellers out of the water. She also wants Ivon Bates tailed. So—as I understand the problem—if our sales go down, the cash flow peters down, and Delmar, our distinguished bean counter and tightwad, cannot pay the interest on the bonds sinking fund."

He looked around and he drew some blank stares.

"I've heard of sinking funds," said Beasley, "if you can't ante up they lend you the funds, like them loan sharks do, till you're sunk."

Ed Wesley added: "That's why I keep my savings in a pass-book account."

"And I hand half of my paycheck to my bookie," said Morales, in a tone of sarcasm in his voice. "My life is a success story: from rags-to-roaches, from Black Harlem to Spanish Harlem, then from Hell's Kitchen to Washington Heights…where the only highs people get are from high rents and crack."

Lowmax looked at Morales and sneered, a malicious sneer that said: "And who asked you to choose to live in miserable unblessed ghettoes, you whining Puerto Rican wetback?"

Lowmax turned to Beasley and said, "Zach, you and Morales spend a couple of days in Jersey around the Bates plant, case the place, poke around, pick up some gossip we can use. Walk around Delphi and get a feel for the layout of the Plant." And an afterthought: "Take that good-looking uniform who's been trying to prove himself. Let him pump the broads at the plant."

Morales asked, "Orlando Finzicontini?"

"Yeah, he likes to be called Danny better than Orlando. He was in the Gulf War with the Navy SEALs. And even though he got kicked out, he still has all that extensive training in explosives. Listen, Ed, since he—Danny Finzicontini — is spinning his wheels, why don't you put him on surveillance detail at the LIC plant? I bet he'll catch them kids, the burglars."

Ed Wesley said. "I'll arrange it with Human Resources."

Smiling with a crooked smile that did little to hide his crooked intentions and crooked teeth, he said, "All right, guys. You—Zach and Freddy—are now on special assignment. I'm budgeting $200 a day for expenses: tips, treats, sucker bets, payola—spreading around money." Without wasting time, he dispensed the money as well as his insidious smile. As they left, Lowmax shook his head, murmuring between his teeth:

"I hope these two dim-witted screwballs bring hot news. What am I to expect from 'Zach of Shit' and 'Freddy Kruger'? I bet Helen gets a big kick out of these nicknames."

Never had he felt so much pressure. "Helen McCain can turn up the heat, that tough demented woman. Hot Damn! I gotta deliver something, at least some kind of plan, even if it is a half-baked plan—or she'll be riding my ass like my cheap underwear!

* * * *

Since Tuesdays were always busy at the Bates Plant, the laborers counted on overtime pay, and treated themselves to full meals at Daniela's. Cowboy, Miss Meneses's assistant Tony Lisanti, Felix, and Lenny were sharing a table. Tony was a pleasant middle-aged man with a contagious loud laugh that people liked. Being an inveterate cruel teaser, Tony enjoyed tormenting Stevie, the waiter. He'd say, "Stevie, you look so cute with that short apron. It really fits you like a miniskirt. And the way you look at Joey with those big Bambi eyes, I bet he's got the hots for you. Don't tell me you were making eyes at Lenny—he's ugly." And Felix: "Be nice, Tony; Stevie is like my son, and soon to graduate from Parsons School of Design."

Cowboy and his cohorts left at about two p.m. Soon after, Stevie saw Hog and Dion Loco Bromius coming across the parking lot. Stevie shouted, "Daniela darling, guess who's coming to dinner?"

"Who?"

"Your two favorite sons: Hog and Loco Bromius."

Two seconds later Hog and Dion sauntered in, talking loudly, jostling each other, and as if on cue, they started blowing kisses and hassling Stevie.

"Hey Stevie, still taking ballet lessons?" Putting his wrists on his hips, palms outward, Hog daintily pranced around, sashaying up and down.

"Leave him alone, Hog," said Loco in a mocking voice, "he is liable to pluck a stiff eyelash and stab you in the ass."

Some catcalling and hooting followed.

Then, as if they had rehearsed the move, they bumped hips twice and slapped a high-five.

Daniela shouted from the kitchen: "You guys lay off if you want to stay! You, Hog, I'm going to remember your being a smart ass the next time you're hungry and come begging for left overs. And you Bromius, I still have an open tab you need to settle up."

Heeding Daniela's outburst, they both shut up, and headed towards the pool table. When they were out of Daniela's range of vision, Hog turned around and mugged with grotesque but quiet twitches at the onlookers. And right behind him, Loco made a slow, long jerk-off gesture with his right hand. Rolling their eyes, two bespectacled, tweeded, middle-aged men—professors at Hudson County Community College—continued their conversation. In a minute, the clicking of the balls resonated throughout the restaurant.

A while later, Orbis' Deputy Chief Zach Beasley and Sergeant Freddy Morales walked in. Surveying the premises with keen eyes, they walked around Raul—the dish washer—who was mopping up the front section, swinging a heavy mop side to side, leaving a mirror-like glint on the floor as he moved down.

Placing his Nikon 35mm camera on the table, Freddy Morales saw that his boss, Chief Crazy-Hose Beasley, was ogling Stevie's back as he minced away, swaying his hips. Morales had shot an entire roll of film when they cased the Bates Plant. And now, while Morales was changing the roll of film, Beasley was drawing a crude diagram of the main buildings and roads. They were on their second round of beers when Beasley asked Stevie: "Is there more than one pool table in the back?"

"Two. A couple of clowns are using one. I'll get you some quarters."

They ambled down to the back and in a short time, Beasley connected with Hog and Dion Loco Bromius. Beasley ordered a round of beers. "I'm treating my pals here—let's play a foursome!" After a while, Morales got tipsy, asking Beasley to stop for a while and sit down at a table to talk about their business.

"Say Hog, Dion…want something to eat, guys?" asked Beasley. "Something light," said Dion.

Hog squealed: "Speak for yourself, Loco! I can eat a full dinner now."

Loco yelled, "Pig! You eat a full dinner at breakfast, at lunch, and at dinner, and if you were a bugger chap Brit, you would eat dinner at tea-time, too!"

Ordering sandwiches, chips, and some water to wash down the bitter taste that the beer had left in their mouths, Beasley asked them to sit down.

Hog asked, "You guys are private investigators—PIs, right?"

"No way," retorted Beasley. "We're insurance investigators. We're undercover…fact-finding, nothing big. Routine stuff." Beasley explained, "Whenever a corporation takes out large fire, theft, and liability policy, we have to make sure everything checks out. We're checking Bates Pharmaceuticals."

"My pal here, Dion Loco Bromius, will tell you all you want to know…all your little heart's desires. He used to work in the Vitamins section till he got fired!"

"Shut up Hog! What's in it for me?"

"Good information is valuable to us, buddy. We could pay you a consultant's fee of, say, a hundred bucks for…"

Barely were the words out of Beasley's mouth when Loco Bromius counter proposed, "Make it two hundred and I'll even draw you a map of every little nook and cranny in the plant!"

"One fifty, but the map's gotta be good."

Stevie kept busy bringing in round after round. On one trip,

Beasley gave Stevie a subtle goose, Stevie's eyes widening in surprise, unable to retaliate. On the next trip, as he was leaning over and pouring beer into a frosted glass, Beasley—unable to control himself—grabbed and squeezed Stevie's buttocks.

Lifting his metal tray and clunking Beasley on the top of his pointed shiny dome, he said, "Don't you get fresh—you're not my type!"

Hog belched.

Loco scolded him, "Excuse yourself, you retard. We're with decent insurance executives. You have no manners, man. You ain't never gonna amount to nothing!"

"Lighten up, man," Morales snapped. "Hog's my buddy."

Hearing that, Hog's eyes fogged up as if in gratitude as he mumbled under his breath, "Puerto Ricans ain't that bad."

When Stevie came to clear the table, Beasley leered and said, "Say, Stevie, you look like you got a good head on your shoulders."

"Yeah?"

"How about a little head, Stevie?"

"Get your head examined, you cone-head, skinhead!" They all laughed at Stevie's outburst. Beasley, too, laughed out loud with clumsy heaving snorts. "That Stevie's a feisty one. Ain't he? I like them when they fight."

Staggering along the steam table toward the door, Beasley—who was at the rear—looked at Stevie with sad eyes and said,

"No hard feelings, huh Stevie? Please smile. C'mon, I want to see that lovely smile. It was only a game…kidding around, Stevie—don't you have a sense of humor? Don't you like to play?"

Stevie softened and smiled. "Well, yes, I do kid around and play…"

"In that case, how about some foreplay, Stevie?"

"Go play with your foreskin, pervert!" Out they went.

Only after he closed the door behind them did Stevie remark to Daniela: "These guys give me the creeps. I can't get over the way they hit it off. I don't get this male bonding; it's beyond me. That big red-necked ape with no eyebrows is a beast, a brute, and a monster. That thick neck! Did you notice the size of his arms? He has thunder thighs for arms! They're up to no good."

"You must tell Sabino."

"No, no, no, dear! You tell him." His voice quivering with

fear, “The old man scares me to death, too! Every time he comes in he seems to bring an icy cloud that hangs around the table all day long. I’ve never seen him talk to anyone…such a diehard loner!”

# Chapter 14 — Grand Rounds

On Thursday of the following week, Dr. Bates returned to the Plant. Dr. Annie Norris, Tom Stone, Sabino, and Dr. Bates met at the front offices and marched to make the weekly grand round. Tom would lead the discussions with the division managers. Dr. Bates was happy to hear that Miss Meneses had the new J.I.T. system—Just in Time inventory—up and running. "No more clipboards, Ivon. These are radio frequency scanners." Impressed by Miss Meneses' prodigious memory, Ivon thought her mind was a huge catalog of production lot numbers, quality control schedules, raw materials, works in progress, and finished products. A fine woman indeed! Steady in work habits and bearing, but doesn't she look grave and austere the way she wears her hair up in a bun? A no-nonsense lady in a position of responsibility is a great asset.

When they reached Bottling, Dr. Loomis joined them, but since Vince Ganoza, the foreman, was out sick, they moved on to VTP: Vitamins, Tablets, and Pills. Young Doctor Bates watched Janos. Oh, yes, Janos Panko, the foreman: a burly man—a barroom brawler. After Joe Bates's murder, Janos had become more aggressive, bossing around even workers in other sections and departments. Is he bucking for Tom's job?

For some time, Miss Meneses and Janos had become rivals, competing for the best run department, but the contest—because of a nasty incident—had turned into a bad-blood feud. Discovering that one lot of vitamins had never made it to storage, Miss Meneses reported the shortage to Tom, who held Janos accountable. To Janos' relief, a few days later, he received an anonymous note accusing Dion Loco Bromius—a wise guy, a shirker and a troublemaker—of the theft. Janos had grabbed one of Loco's ankles and Brick the other and together they had dragged the screaming thief to Tom's office, where Pia had confronted Janos for his brutality.

The workers often talked about Pia having the hots for Loco, for they often saw her touch his face, ruffle his hair, hug him, and when she thought she was unobserved, she'd kiss the cherry mark on his forehead. Tom fired Dion Loco Bromius on the spot despite Pia's tears and hysterical protests. Many people at the plant could never understand why Tom had hired him, and the general rumor was that Pia had somehow twisted Tom Stone's arm; that she had something on him.

After the rounds, Dr. Bates, Tom, and Dr. Norris spoke for a while in Tom's office, later going to Daniela's for lunch. Daniela's was on Tonnelle Avenue, next to Florence's Fresh Flowers, south of Bolton's Hardware Store and Polly Wanna Cracker pet store. Victor Feng drove them to the restaurant, which was the only decent eatery in the area, and where the Bates workers had lunch and supper, when they had to work overtime. After Stevie took their order, which included a bottle of red wine, Tom Stone started the conversation. "Since you mentioned your plans to get a Deputy Plant Manager, you should know that in another six months I'll be sixty-five, and Sabino is even older than me; I need to train this deputy."

"Do you have any ideas about someone from within…Janos?"

"You're not serious, Ivon!" exclaimed Annie Norris, who disliked even the mere mention of the name.

Tom shook his head. "Janos? No way. I was thinking of Miss Meneses." Annie Norris nodded. "I endorse Tom's choice."

Dr. Bates' eyes glittered with approval. "I guess in your own way you've been grooming her all these years—right, Tom? And I agree. I have a lot of respect for her; even dad addressed her as Miss Meneses. Cheers!"

"But shouldn't we develop Janos? Send him to some workshops and seminars for line managers?"

"All that is okay," said Annie Norris, "but you can't change human nature. Janos is too narrow-minded, pigheaded, and abusive! And that drooling idiot Brick—his cousin and sidekick—that covers his back and laughs at his jokes is even worse. I've seen a few broken blood vessels on the tip of his nose: a sign of booze for sure and I am afraid the man is an alcoholic, too."

Annie's sultry voice lingered in Dr. Bates' ears and he felt his face get hot; a strange thrill filled his heart with lust. And aren't you, dear Doctor Norris, a fine woman, too? She sees what ordinary people can't see, and that's the strangeness that gives her that glow. A beauty in her own right, but watch out, boy—the woman could be is bad news! The thought of Annie demanding co-ownership of the patent deflated his delicious stirring and destroyed the delightful feverish longing.

Stevie brought a second bottle of Merlot.

"My father always said that people are the key to success in business: that is, good people. His favorite saying was, 'you need a good team of horses to pull the wagon.'"

"Your father hired me and Dr. Loomis here in Jersey, but Sabino and your old man had been together since Vietnam," said Tom. "Joe got a commission as a major—being a graduate from MIT. He and Sabino were POWs and escaped together."

"Father was a driven man."

"Your father was always in a rush to make a buck: 'Pay your bills on time and collect your receivables on time.' Well, he had no problems with the cash flow. If someone fell behind in his payments, your father would send Sabino and Sabino always collected—don't ask me how. That Sabino is some tough hombre, I'll tell you."

"I grew up listening to Sabino's stories and often I hear his voice and mine — as a child—and the chats we used to have. I still recall the first day he let me explore the swamp. He never liked to talk about his own exploits, but once in a while he'd yield. Father told me Sabino saved his life during the Tet Offensive in Vietnam, but Sabino never wanted to talk about war."

"I've also heard about the Cuban Marielitos and the Colombian Mafia. I'm hoping he told you about it...did he?" asked Tom.

"It's a scary story—I'll share with you some other time."

"I hear Joey De Lemos is as tough as Sabino," said Dr. Norris, who unaccustomed to wine, was slurring her words. "That wild blond kid is a noble creature—*creecherrr*—and he doesn't know it!"

Hmm, another insight, by this lovely unravished maiden, thought Ivon and he smiled inwardly as he pictured himself undoing the buttons of her pristine-white blouse, exposing her breasts and nestling his head in her bosom. He wondered if the blow from those hoodlums—a mild concussion; the doctor had said—had made him more lecherous.

"Here, have more wine," said he, wishing to see her drunk.

"Hic, *yeshhh*h—*thanky, Ivy*."

"Anyway, won't Joey, wild as he is, be hard to manage?" asked Dr. Bates.

"Wild stallions make good workhorses, Ivon. Besides, I promised Sammy-Lee, his mom, before she died that I'd look after him. Poor Sammy-Lee! She drank herself to death. She did her college internship here at the lab, and when she graduated from Rutgers University, your father hired her as a chemist."

The sudden ring of Tom's cell phone startled them.

"Lenox Davis woke up screaming out of his mind…the hospital…"

With a rush in his voice, Dr. Bates said, "Let's go see him right now." Since Ketty had told him that people in the Plant and in the main offices were saying how compassionate, how sincere, and how caring he was with his workers, he felt he should go again.

* * * *

"You might not remember me, Mr. Stone," said Nurse Pritchard, "but you used to come by the Bates Ward. I saw you and Mr. Hepplewhite, our director, several times." Then she told them about Lenox's adverse reaction to the painkillers, but that he was stable now. "Orbis Laboratories products are unreliable; in particular, that painkiller they sell should be off the market!" Ivon made a mental note to speak to Alex Panagora to find out why the Orbis products were in use here, and not the generic Bates painkillers. As they went into the room, they saw Lenox was napping, snoring with occasional muscle spasms. The young African-American man who had been sitting down stood up.

Nurse Pritchard said, "Sleep is the best medicine—catnaps. He'll wake up soon; meanwhile, talk to Mr. Davis' son, this strong young man here."

Tom sympathized. "The important thing is that he's out of danger."

"Either he developed immunity to the painkillers or that damned drug is defective. Dr. Spinnell can't be sure," said Nurse Pritchard, and she withdrew.

Gazing at Lenox, Jr., Dr. Bates sized him up. Lenox, Jr. was 6 feet, 3 or 4 inches, around 240 pounds and maybe 22 or 23 years old. Bleached dreadlocks. A stiff, matted tress dangled and quavered between his eyes, touching the tip of his nose. "Did you play football, Lenox?" Ivon asked him.

Lenox, Jr. grinned. "I tried, but I washed out with the 49ers, the Houston Oilers, the Giants, and a couple of months ago with the Jets."

"Too bad," said Tom and he scratched his bulbous nose. "Will you try again? Maybe the Patriots?"

"No, that's it for me. I had my chance. Coaches said I didn't have the killer instinct, but the truth is I never had a passion for it in college. In fact, I liked books better than football, and that is a no-no when you are on a football scholarship. I even did homework and wrote term papers!"

"Your father is going to be out for a long time," said Tom. "We've got opportunities for young people at the plant. We need career personnel. Not fly-by-night people or transients who don't care for their employers."

Junior's eyes showed genuine surprise. "Are you offering me a job, sir?" He took a step back and looked at his father, who was still asleep.

Dr. Bates nodded. "Not a job, Lenox. A career—lifetime employment." Tom continued, "Dr. Bates is going to restructure the company. To begin with, we don't have a Logistics Department and, in these times, we can't compete without people with skills in transportation schedules, cargo, sea, air, surface, rail, and so on. We need to build up several other departments, too, and for that we need people we can trust, like family. Stop by my office tomorrow and we'll talk more. You may start right away unless you have other plans."

So bent and absorbed had they been in their talk that they had not heard Lenox's low moans and whispers. Lenox rasped, "I see you met Junior."

Junior whispered in the old man's ear, and Lenox's eyes widened. "Thanks, Tom," he said smiling, "I lived with the fear that one of them sailors would hurt Junior in that stupid part-time job. Did he tell you he's a bouncer at a whore-house on the Bayonne waterfront?"

Lenox, Jr. grinned.

"Yes, he mentioned it," Tom lied.

After a mild attack of a wheezing cough, Lenox signaled Junior to crank up the bed. Lenox Jr. found the cable with the control buttons, and pressing the 'Up' button, the bed—with a muffled rumble—lifted at an angle. Fluffing the pillows and then—unconcerned about appearances and with great tenderness—Junior kissed his father's forehead.

"Junior is a big man. He can take care of himself, let me tell you. But against a bunch of liquored-up Norwegians, Filipinos, Greeks, or crazy South Afrikaners? Them horny merchant marines are tough brothers."

"Ain't that bad, Pa; besides, they never carry guns."

"Still, it ain't right. No, it ain't right for a college man to work as a bouncer in a waterfront whorehouse."

"No more, Pa. I got a regular job now."

Touching Lenox's shoulder, Dr. Bates said, "I'm a couple of years older than you; but I remember seeing you around the Plant when we were kids. You, Lenox, and my father worked together for many years; now I'm looking forward to working with Lenox, Jr.—one generation follows the other."

# Chapter 15 — Debates and Rebates

Tossing a bulging laundry bag into the back seat of the Impala, Joey watched Sabino train his Doberman Pinschers. So that's how the old man keeps in such great shape! From his safe distance, he saw the danger packed in the dogs' muscles and jaws, and he wondered who was more dangerous, the master or the dogs.

Because he admired Sabino, he felt an ardor to rise in the world. He, Joey D. De Lemos, would amount to something one day. Mother went to the Rutgers School of Pharmacy; maybe that's the key: go to college too. Must ask Tom Stone. He's a wise man, a military man and has a kind heart. Tom treated him with kindness, and it made him wonder if Tom and his mom…maybe. No, no, it ain't possible! Besides, he is black…. you never know. What about Sabino?

A vile gust of miasma lashed out of the swamp, burning his face, lodging in his nostrils, making him wonder about those misty marshes, the whirlpool, the quicksand. The swamp holds a particular charm; it feels alluring and yet spooky. In his dreams, he'd hear the spirits of the woods calling him, telling him his mother was a goddess and that he was the heir of the woods. He would see himself frolicking, roaming, dancing and floating through the woods dressed in fawn-skins, crowned with ivy.

A time will come to check out the swamp. For now, let's see what's doing in Union City, feeling that it was going to be a wild night. Cowboy had frequented the Istanbul Boutique to court Lisa, now that she had broken up with Dion Bromius.

* * * *

While Cowboy was explaining to Mr. Naxos, the tailor—a middle-aged, gray-haired man with thick glasses—what he wanted done, the white gauzy curtains that separated the shop from the back room parted, and a young woman appeared. What do we have here? Her physical beauty stunned Cowboy: large emerald-green eyes, sensuous unpainted lips, perfect line-thin eyebrows, black hair falling to her shoulders in thick glimmering ringlets. Man, those eyes! She was wearing dark brown pants and an immaculate white blouse with long sleeves.

Reaching for his tape, the tailor took the measurements, but the young woman stepped in, and taking the tape from him she said: "I'll do it, dad." Looking at her long, tapering fingers, he touched her hand and said, "You have the hands of a goddess."

"Thanks, you are kind," the young woman said, lowering her eyes for a second. "Your eyes tell me you're searching for something. But don't you know you are what you will become?"

How does she sound so old, being so young? Feeling a lustful pang, Cowboy wanted to hold her and kiss her. Had the old man not been there, perhaps he would have been more aggressive.

She said, "I'll have everything ready tomorrow afternoon…is that soon enough?"

Hearing her sweet voice, his libido rose like a pitched tent.

A few minutes later, he swaggered along Bergenline Avenue toward the Istanbul Boutique, and as he turned to the alley, he saw Lisa and Hog locking up the store. Cowboy kissed Lisa and turning, he slapped Hog on the shoulder.

"Where's your car, Mr. Industrialist Bates?" asked Hog.

"I parked by Sloan's. I had to take some clothes to the Naxos shop." "Oh yeah, aha, aha," teased Hog.

Lisa said, "All right, Cowboy, I guess you met Ariana, right? Ari was the brains of the class in high school. She writes poems that appear in the local newspapers and in some magazines, and she has already published a collection as a book. A gentle dreamer."

Turning to Hog, he asked him, "Since you know the way to Alfonse's, you drive, okay Hog?"

"Okay, if you buy me a hamburger. There's a brand-new McDonald's in West New York. Since I have to watch my diet, all I need is a small little hamburger; I ain't pigging out no more. Is that okay, Cowboy?"

"Okay with me, Hog. You didn't have lunch?" asked Cowboy.

"Or breakfast! These are ugly days, my man. Since Lou caught Dion Loco Bromius stealing jewelry from the store, Lou's been in a bad mood. I am afraid to be around him. He don't let no one go in the back of the store no more, and he don't let me crash upstairs no more, neither."

"Dion is such a bad influence, Hog," said Lisa. "You'll pay for his stupid cons and crimes."

"If he keeps calling me a retard, I won't hang out with him no more."

Since Cowboy and Lisa weren't hungry, they had coffee. But Hog changed his mind, and instead of the little hamburger, he had a Big Mac with extra cheese and bacon, large fries, and a large Coke, no ice, please—and toss in that apple pie, too, my man. They watched him eat his full meal as well as his words.

"I have no place to stay," said Hog. "I'm in a such a jam! One day I'm gonna get me a steady job and I'll have my pad: that's my wish. That's not asking for much, is it, Cowboy?"

"Not at all, Hog," said Cowboy.

"Listen, your eyes are going to pop when you see Alfonse's display. Fantastic, beautiful pieces." Hog smiled. "You gonna like my pal, Alfonse. You gonna be happy I'll introduce—*introjuice*—you to him."

Lisa tensed up. "I don't know why you guys get so worked up about these things. I guess they make you feel more macho, more secure, more…so that you can be more like in your face. But let me tell you, these things are nothing but trouble."

Being familiar with the area, in no time Hog found the corner of the corner of Edgewater and River Road. Going through the revolving door, Cowboy, Lisa, and Hog stepped up to the doorman at the reception desk. "He's waiting for you guys," the man said. "Go right ahead—push 'P' for penthouse."

Cowboy found Alfonse courteous and well mannered, a handsome man in his mid-thirties, with a voice of a network anchorman. A large Maurice Villency lacquered wall unit displayed a mix of firearms. Cowboy thought a 9mm Smith & Wesson revolver was what he needed for protection.

"Let me see it," said Cowboy. "Nice piece!" He smelled it, tucked it in his waist, put it in his pants pockets, then in his jacket pocket.

"Ammo?"

Alfonse handed him two magazines with free ammo. Hog said to Cowboy, "Dinn, I tell you Alfonse was cool?" He turned to Alfonse, "say Alfonse, could I crash here for the night? Lou's been in a bitchy mood, and he won't let me stay at his place anymore."

"What happened?"

"Lou caught Dion stealing jewelry from the store," said Lisa. "Now Lou don't want anybody hanging around the store and his place."

“Hog, you better stay away from that guy, Dion. I hear he is a follower of Donato Sabellius, the leader of a weird vampire cult. They're into Bloody Metal, body piercing, blood drinking, stoning and black masses. These creeps will get you in trouble. The reason I know Donato's name is that he had the nerve to send me a letter soliciting a donation for his church from me. Tax free and all that jazz."

Hog said, “I'm slow, but not stupid. Donato scares the living lights out of me. Like he's a ghost or something."

“I've heard rumors he's sworn to destroy the Bates Plant," said Alfonse. “Yeah, Donato claims his parents died, maybe killed, in a fire there at the Bates Plant," said Hog. “Still, I think Dion Loco is even more dangerous than Donato—he's a psycho. One day at a bus stop, Dion yanked the purse of an old lady, knocked her to the ground and then kicked her face and ribs to shut her up 'cause she was screaming at the top of her lungs."

“You may stay here, Hog—tonight."

Since it was after 11 p.m. and they were getting hungry, Lisa gave directions to Cowboy to the Napalm Alley—a honky-tonk bar-restaurant—where they could have something to eat and have a good time. Lisa explained Lou owned the business. “They know me there, so we'll eat something and at no charge."

In a few minutes they got there, parked, and followed a gravel path, trailing a young couple heading to the same place. As soon as they opened the door, they heard a blast of loud music and voices. The bar's sign read Napalm Alley, and except for the glow of the beer signs, the entrance was dark. Cowboy followed Lisa, who, knowing the place well, weaved through tables, traversing the dance floor to get to the bar. The bartender's eyes widened with surprise. “Well, what brings you to our neck of the woods, Lisa?"

“Long time no see, Nam! This is Joey De Lemos, a friend of Lou's."

Cowboy felt Nam's strong grip. You can tell a man by his handshake. Often a handshake reveals more than a person's eyes, and it ain't hard to see that my man's had his share of suffering. Nam wore his long hair in a ponytail—a gray limp ponytail. Lisa ordered pastrami sandwiches and a pitcher of beer. “And bring some pickles on the side, Nam."

As they sat at the table to the right of the bar, they saw three couples slow dancing to a plaintive Country Western song,

Forever my love, forever my darling

I'll love you till the end of the night.

That must be an awful long night, thought Cowboy. These country songs are strange, but never too sour or too sweet. The place felt homey, and after Alfonse's Art déco penthouse, this place was just fine: thick scratched-up oak tables, sturdy straight-back chairs, and sawdust-covered floors. They ate and drank a second pitcher of beer, and then they heard a fast, loud tune fill the air. Clasping Lisa's hand, Cowboy guided her to the dance floor where he cut loose, showing off with some fancy cool steps. Since his dancing was dazzling and contagious, many other couples dashed to the floor where they all joined up in a frenetic dancing whirl.

It was almost midnight.

The dance floor was jumping and throbbing, with fresh couples joining in, some jitterbugging, others heeling, tipping, and clapping. At the bar, Nam was sliding mugs and passing glasses behind his back; quick hands, man. At midnight, Nam started clanging a large metal triangle that hung from the ceiling; he banged it with a wild, mad insistence.

"C'mon buffalo chips, drink up! Don't forget to ante up for my pension plan."

He pushed the huge fish bowl.

"And don't put no coins there, man. My 401 (K) accepts bills only, and don't be cheap tossing in 'georgies'—toss in some upscale faces there, man. You're a hustler, Nam. Get a job! By the time we baby-boomers try to collect our social insecurity retirement pension, it ain't gonna be there…So chip in you cheapies!"

The Napalm Alley became an intoxicated reality.

After a long while, the Napalm Alley settled down, not with marked abruptness but with ebbing ease. And when Cowboy and Lisa were about to leave, Nam came to the table and whispered into Lisa's ear. Cowboy bristled, adrenaline flowing through his blood, as a strange irrational warning filled his body—not his brain.

In the next instant, he saw Dion Loco Bromius and three scraggly half-drunk goons step up to the table. Dion glared at Lisa and barked in her face, "Stupid whore, what are you doing here with this faggot? I told you I'd be in touch—couldn't wait, huh?"

"You're drunk, Dion," said Lisa. "I want nothing to do with you, ever!"

"We're goan teach lover boy here a lesson he'll never forget, then I'm gonna take you home."

A slender man—the leader of the group—with lank, unwashed, frowzy blond hair that lay flat on his shoulders smiled, baring sharp fangs. He wore a black short mid-riff tank top under his black leather jacket, his pale face glowing with unnatural light lips twisting in an evil smile. Cowboy couldn't help thinking that if he was close enough to him, he would smell blood on his breath.

Rushing to the table as if to avert a fight, Nam said, "C'mon, Dion…Donato, please talk to Dion. Let's have a good time. No sense in stirring up trouble."

Fascinated, not by Loco Bromius—whom he already knew was a loudmouth petty criminal—but by Donato's ease of manner and movement on the ill-lit side, he kept quiet. The feeble lights and gloom made Donato look unnatural—a ghost. He watched Donato say something to Dion Loco Bromius and then to the goons. Donato's eyes and teeth glittered in the dark, making Cowboy squirm. So, this is the famous Donato, Donato Sabellius: wise and well-traveled, young, yet he smells of the ages, of coffins, of decay, and sin and perversion. He could wash that greasy hair…disgusting, revolting. Something ain't human about him—a monster. Much to his relief, he saw Donato and his group ebb away toward a dark corner.

Pleased, Nam said, "Thanks, guys. Drinks on the house." No sooner had Nam said that than a rowdy group barged in through the front door. A tall wiry man, who removing his topcoat with an operatic air, handed it to the bee-hived woman standing to his right, seemed to be the leader. Who's this dude with the cheap business suit? No tie, seedy shirt. Cowboy saw Dion Loco Bromius rush to greet the dude and to shake hands. Dion whispered in his ear and the tall man bobbed his head as though he were getting the picture of what Dion was saying.

Taking a few steps toward Nam, the tall wiry man said, "My

cousin Dion Bromius tells me he has a score to settle with this queer here. I want to make sure you stay out of it, Nam"

"Come on, Coz. Everything is cool. Why don't…"

"Shut up!" screamed the drooly goon. In a shrill voice, Dion Loco Bromius yelled, "Yeah, shut up, Nam! This is between me and this punk." Nam backed off, his gray ponytail quavering against the soft glow of the bar lights. Dion stepped up to Cowboy's booth again, and the two goons closed ranks behind him. Keeping aloof, as though not wishing to get involved, Donato gazed at the crowd with languid indifference, as if violence bored him. Coz stood to the right of them, glowering at Nam.

Looking at Dion with contempt, Cowboy's eyes focused on Coz, sizing him up, making out that pompadour and the ridiculous lamb-chop sideburns.

Man, it's so quiet!

Cowboy saw a shape unplug the old-fashioned Wurlitzer jukebox. The women and men in the raucous group stood frozen, as if nailed to the dance floor. At the tables, silhouettes sat erect, tense, watchful. Feeling his senses alive, Cowboy sighed with a sense of resignation. Here we are, chilling out and these turds come to stink up the place. There it is! His thigh rubbed against Lisa's legs and he felt Lisa's trembling knees tap against his thigh.

Dion shrieked, "Get up, you chickenshit!"

"Stay where you are, Dion, you'll live longer," ordered Cowboy in a chilling undertone.

With a look at the goons that was an appeal for support, Dion stuck his hand in his black jeans pocket, pulled a set of large brass knuckles, and fitted them on his right hand. Only when Dion Loco Bromius stepped in did Cowboy spring to his feet with a feline motion, his extended right arm looking abnormally long. The two goons froze, their eyes shining with fear, as Cowboy held the Smith & Wesson right between Dion's eyes.

"You know, Dion…that earring doesn't look too cool on you—I'm going to fix it for you."

Lisa's lips were twitching, as if in prayer: please put the gun away, God.

"If I ever see your face again, I will fix your other ear and make you swallow those brass knuckles." He raked the gun over Dion's face and pointed it to the left ear. Cowboy pulled the gun about an inch away, but just in that precise instant Dion—whether by accident or from fear—dropped the brass knuckles, which in the dead silence of the night hit the floor with a loud, flat clang.

The gun crackled with a deafening blast, hurling Dion Loco Bromius backward toward the arms of the two goons, splattering them with blood and bits of ear cartilage. The muzzle flash scorched the left side of Dion's face, leaving it wrinkled and dark gray, like wet elephant skin.

Oblivious to Dion's squirming and howling, Cowboy trained the gun on Coz: "I feel I know you, Coz—or you know me. Or maybe I've seen you before."

"Never met you, man. Ain't got no personal beef with you, man."

"Well, you called me queer. I'm straight, and even if I was gay—that'd be my private right, my God-given free will. It's you bigots and religious fanatics who are the curse of the human race. Wanna call me queer again?"

Squirming and by now cowed, Coz looked at Donato as if appealing for help, but Donato lowered his eyes, unwilling to commit himself. Coz—his voice now reedy and flaky—all but begged, "Let it go, let me buy you a beer, no hard feelings, let it go, okay, bud?"

Taking that as an apology, he let it go and stuck the gun in his pocket. To think that only a few minutes ago Coz had been so macho, and now he's shaking in his boots. Feeling weary, he wanted to get away and go to sleep and forget the violence of the night. "Let's go Lisa, Babe. I'm sorry I dragged you into this mess." As they headed toward the door, Cowboy and Nam slapped hands across the bar and a bond formed between them. Cowboy said, "There it is, buddy!"

"There it is!" replied Nam.

Having cojones simply means that after all is said and done, only one fact remains: that no one can die for you.

# Chapter 16 — Helen McCain returns

On Sunday evening, Helen McCain returned from Washington D.C. The next morning, getting up one hour earlier than usual, she drew herself a deep warm bath. What a delight! Taking her time, she rubbed her thighs and hips with a washrag while she breathed in the warm lilac-scented water, an erotic scent that made her feel sensuous. Next, she soaped her heavy breast and caressed it with tender fingers. She kept rubbing it and squeezing it and soon she felt aroused, reclining in a languid pose, uttering low moans. Oh, Lord, how she missed her right breast. She ran the washrag over the crumpled scar tissue from where her right breast had been, having lost it to cancer over twenty years ago. Damn cancer! Damn estrogen level used to go off the charts, that's why…But, no! Too busy to attend to the lump…no lumpectomy…letting that mutant gene romp wild. What the hell, this one is still hard. Mucho macho Joe Bates used to go goggled-eyed and drooly over them.

Imagine poor little me falling in love with a monster! No doubt Joe was a monster.

Plucking a few obstinate wiry long hairs that had grown under her chin, she then cut her toenails, placing the parings on the edge of the settee, scooping them up and dropping them into the toilet. Selecting a black prosthetic bra, a black slip and hose, and a pinstriped pantsuit, she dressed with fastidious care. Twenty minutes later, she strode past the reception desk.

"How is it outside, Orson?" she asked the doorman.

"Kinda slippery, Ms. McCain. Be careful."

Reaching the south corner of St. Patrick's Cathedral and seeing the sidewalk in front of the Cathedral was clean, she hastened her pace, the coarse grains of salt crunching under the fine soles of her pumps. As she touched her wrist, she noticed that her watch wasn't there. Shoes in fecal matter—forgot my watch! Darn, aren't we humans creatures of habit? If so, how did this annoying lapse happen?

Orbis Laboratories' corporate offices were on Fifty-sixth, about mid- block between Fifth Avenue and Avenue of the Americas. Passing the Orbis building on to the corner of Fifty-sixth and Seventh Avenue, she stopped at the bank to draw some pocket money from the ATM. Whether it was clumsiness—as her hands were icy-cold—or from the whims of digital automation, the dumb machine rejected her code. In disgust, she pummeled several keys, causing the screen to blank out. Damn—it swallowed my card! She departed toward the office sneezing, fuming, humorless, and cashless.

Of all the people riding the elevator with her, she distinguished a middle-aged woman in a wheelchair and a well-dressed young woman holding a red plastic folder against her bosom. Resumes. Nodding as if appreciating the young woman's presence and good looks, McCain smiled, and the young woman reciprocated. McCain thought: Aha, going for an interview! Good luck, my little chickadee. Excellent appearance, great legs, high breasts—bet her breast ducts are squeaky clean! Oh, yes, let's have a look at her shanks. Wow! Let's hope we have something upstairs in the attic. The young woman's eyes shined with the spark of intelligence. Focusing on a woman in a wheelchair, she remarked to herself, why doesn't that ugly woman—taking up half of the space in the elevator—stay home? And that worn out bag she's clutching must be full of inhumanities.

A sudden jolt and jarring noise in the elevator shaft drew her out of her musings. McCain cursed. "Damn—the damned elevator broke again!"

"My luck. I'm going to be late for my interview. My luck!" cried the young lady, appealing to McCain for sympathy.

"Not to worry," the CEO empathized. "I'll walk you to Personnel and I will explain the delay."

Desperate, the young woman stamped her foot. "Oh no, I have a third crucial interview with Mr. Henry Cook. Not Human Resources, not Personnel—Mr. Cook!"

"Not to worry. I'll explain what happened to him. I'm Mr. Cook's boss."

Only then did the young woman's eyes widened, recognizing Helen McCain. McCain looked at the panel and pushed the red button to sound the alarm. The elevator was stuck between floors, but soon they heard voices from above yelling,

"We'll get it going in a minute. Don't worry, help is on the way." Rumbles of protest followed, the woman in the wheelchair shrieking, "Hurry! I'm claustrophobic."

Removing her coat, the young woman exposed an elegant red

blazer, Helen McCain nodding in approval. A cool cookie, she thought. Red must be this year's black. Having locked eyes, the young woman engaged McCain in conversation. "I'm proud to meet you, Ms. McCain. It took me a couple of minutes, but I recognized you from the covers of Forbes and Fortune," she said with aplomb. "My name is Susan Connelly. I've researched the company and I see that your leadership has made the company what it is today. You engineered all those successful buyouts, terrific market share, ever-increasing earnings per share, and lots of international trade. You're an inspiration to us, being a self-made woman of substance."

Helen McCain forced a smile. "Thank you, Susan. We've plenty of room for growth here for young people. I can't think of a more exciting place than Orbis Laboratories; keep in mind that software, hardware, and pharmaceuticals will be the leaders in the new millennium."

Agitated and searching her bag with frantic fingers, the woman in the wheelchair kept mumbling, "My Xanax…my Xanax." To everyone's relief, the elevator restarted.

Faithful to her promise, McCain guided Susan Connelly to Henry the Eight's office. On her way to her office, she chewed on some suspicious thoughts. Hold it a damned minute! How come this Susie—or a soon-to-be Catherine of Aragon—knows so much about Orbis? Something's rotten in the state of Arkansas! She seems clever and well-spoken; let's hope Henry hires her for her smarts, not her looks. A derriere to plant a flag on…and those luscious thighs! American women are the real challenge of our postmodern age. The problem is that as Americans get older, they get fleshy and dumpy. Dumpy indeed. Forget about those bowlegged and bad-teethed Asian and European women. Orthodontists in those wretched countries starve. What of those Brazilian women who, without a doubt, come second to Americans, but with one definite advantage: they never get dumpy! Americans are becoming a nation of fat wagging rumps. She halted her energetic stride, only to stop as if struck by a revelation.

A dumpsite!

A wonderful dumpsite! Bates Pharmaceuticals owns all that land and a swamp and what a gold mine that could be. Millions and millions of dollars in savings if the swamp is to be used as a chemical dumpsite. Get rid of all the industrial waste that costs so much to transport. Dump it right there in your own backyard. Wow! For Joe Bates and now Ivon to ignore this hidden reservoir of wealth is dereliction of duty. "This is a windfall," she whispered. "And to celebrate, let's break a little wind. Ah, yesssss! Let's enjoy the pleasures of the rectum rectorum sans decorum!"

Watch out for Sabino though, more loyal than a golden retriever, yet more vicious than a Rottweiler crossed with a Pit Bull. Some mutt: half Japanese, half Peruvian! How well did she remember Sabino's threat: "Come near Antonia and that baby and you'll eat quicksand for dinner and eternity." Yet that dangerous man said nothing about coming near the company. Let's hope, she said to herself, Fart-face Lester the Molester has concocted a plan to cripple Bates Pharmaceuticals. She couldn't help mumbling with some relish, Let's move on before I get too dumpy.

* * * *

Buried beneath a financial newsletter, she saw a letter with two full pages of tight text Camilla had set on top of the pile. Glancing at the letterhead, she then flipped it upside down and tossed it in her 'Hold' basket. Focusing on a memo from Delmar Gotti, the V.P. of Finance—the annual request for Christmas bonuses—she despaired. The company can use the money in these tough lean days. Besides, annual bonuses are such an archaic idea—a bonus for everyone rewards both the productive and the dead wood. In our postmodern era, it no longer makes sense. She called Delmar Gotti. "About the bonuses…set aside the same amount as last year's and let Henry dole it out."

"You sure, Helen? You've done this every year, and no one has ever complained, Helen. You've always been fair."

"Let him do it this year." As she hung up, she mumbled, "You jackass!" Neither distractions nor attractions nor other actions could divert her attention from that two-page letter from Randall D. Dodge—a top executive from the largest HMO in New York City—that she had put in the 'Hold" box. With a sudden move, she grabbed it and sped-read it.

Holy caca! Shoes in fecal matter!

What in the name of God is this? The blood draining from her face; she sat frozen, panting, her shoulders—normally tout and pulling at her chest—were now slack and droopy, as if in a defeated stance. Is Randy joking? She rose to her feet as if in a daze and walked over to the mahogany sideboard. Sidling to her right to steady herself against a bookcase and the Chippendale piecrust table, she reached for the fresh pitcher of water. Her hands trembling with Parkinson-like tremors, and spilling water all over the napkins on the tray, she managed to fill the glass. Pulling a plastic cylinder from her jacket pocket, she removed a capsule and swallowed it, drinking the whole glass of water with noisy greedy gulps, the folds of her throat jiggling up and down with each spastic gulp.

To her, problems came in two kinds: human catastrophes and cosmic events. She cleared her throat and murmured, "I've survived worse catastrophes than plagues and HMOs! Damn the HMOs, this is not a cosmic event. This is a temporary setback, and there is no reason to panic. Think and execute with force. Yes, of course, let Lester the Molester execute with all deliberate force. Lester the Molester will have to come through—so let's motivate him." She called Delmar Gotti again.

"Here is what I want you to do. Cut a check for Lester for $25,000."

"$25,000! No security person ever got that much, Helen," whined Delmar.

"Don't worry, Delmar, and I'm happy you're questioning this large check. That's the sign of a good CFO. But trust me, this is a special case. When you have the check ready, hold it and bring it to me. I'll present it to Lester myself."

Only after her medication kicked in did she regain her coolness, and soon she felt ready for action. Even if it means kissing Randy's patrician white bottom, she thought, Empire HMO means millions to Orbis; we can't lose it to Bates.

# Chapter 17 — Annie's research

The following day, Victor drove Ivon to the Midtown Precinct North, on West 51st, where he met with Detective Wilkins. He told Wilkins—in factual detail, neither enhancing nor diminishing the violence he had experienced—the occurrence at the nightclub Stringfellows.

"The second attacker sneaked up behind me and whammo! Lights out."

Detective Wilkins asked him not to file a separate complaint because he felt the incident and the murder belonged together in the same investigation, and that he would add a memo to the case file. He then handed Ivon a copy of a page of old Doctor Bates' appointment book. "Could you or some of your colleagues check that note? Looks like a formula—something you use in the chemical labs—and we can't make much sense out of it. But as I told you, we don't want to leave any stone unturned."

* * * *

Once at the Plant, Dr. Bates headed straight to the labs where he and Dr. Ana G. Norris worked together the whole day. At lunchtime, Ivon showed Dr. Norris the sheet that Detective Wilkins had given him.

"We found this note in father's appointment book. Does it seem familiar to you, Annie?"

"It doesn't look like any of his chemical formulas…maybe something he used in business, like depreciation, inventory ordering… 'C' could stand for cost of capital?"

Ivon nodded. "Thanks, you just gave me an idea." Is there no limit to Annie's intelligence? Who'd expect her to know about those business terms? "I'll ask my friend Beedee—Brian Dedrick, the Marketing and Business professor at Fashion Institute of Technology."

Late in the afternoon, when she hit upon a solution to their experiment, Annie exclaimed, "Ivon, it works, it really works!" The technicians promptly gathered around and, as the word spread, they cheered. Hugging Dr. Norris first and then lifting her off the floor, he twirled her around, exclaiming, "You did it! After the holidays, we're going to farm the project out for human clinical testing," said Dr. Bates. "I'll ask Humana Labs to line up at least 2,000 people in different regions."

Feeling a burst of hope and exultation, he forgot—if not wholly, at least partially—about his other problems, but in particular about the death threat. This was a grueling project for sure and Annie's probably run down, too. When the technicians returned to their stations, he and Dr. Norris walked slowly to her office, and Dr. Norris closed the door behind her.

"It may be wise for you to take the rest of the week off, Annie. The Plant is going to be closed next week, so you might as well get started on your Christmas vacation now. Today's Wednesday and we'll be closed for two weeks, anyway."

"Now that you mention it, I'm really bushed. What a marathon!"

"We've accomplished something for humanity," said Dr. Bates.

"Oh, Ivon. You're so different from your dad. Your father would have said, 'guess what this is going to do to *the bottom line*.' He always put private interest ahead of public purpose. But you always think of others." Looking at him with adoring eyes, she asked him, "Please draw up that co-owner-ship contract. I've spent a great deal of thought and energy and sleepless nights on this project, and you know it was my original idea."

"I will attend to it, Annie. You get started with your time off tomorrow, okay?"

"Thanks, Ivon. It means a great deal to me. It makes me feel confident, worthy, that I am an accomplished woman," she said with a deep sigh. "A few days of peace will do us good. Besides, I can get started writing that paper for the New England Journal of Medicine."

Ivon smiled broadly. "For starters, and after we get the results from Humana Labs, you'll have to send a detailed account of the research to the Proceedings of the National Academy of Sciences, too."

"It's so exciting; I'm looking forward to next year. Are you sure we can afford to spend all that money on research equipment? And there are enormous costs for installation and maintenance, too."

"The company is solid," replied Dr. Bates with a tinge of caution in his voice. "We only have one big loan from a small bank, but Manufacturers Hanover Trust is ready to give me a 5-million-dollar loan. Phil feels I'm being too impulsive, and he isn't happy about it; in fact, he is very unhappy, but I've decided and the equipment is already on its way."

"Oh, Ivon," she said as though she'd had an afterthought. "I saw your picture in the Sunday Times. You look great in a tux…and your date Laura…I forgot her last name…gorgeous in that Versace suit!" Her voice trailed off as if in a throb of hurt.

Whether he felt remorse or joy, he couldn't tell, but his heart quaked, sensing the hurt that her sweet, low voice betrayed. His gaze shifted to her slender hand. "Oh, yes—that was a gala benefit for The Requiem Chorales Association, of which Laura is a member of the Board. She also works for the investment bank that is helping me do the groundwork for some financing. She's only a business acquaintance."

He searched for her face and awkwardly bent his knees, hugging her again and kissing her cheek gently. Dr. Norris peered at him for a second, lowering her gaze, eyelashes fluttering as she delicately blushed. Holding her in his arms, he smelled the faint fragrance she favored. He released her, running his hands down her arms, gently holding her hand. A lovely woman indeed! Feeling his breath quicken, he let go of her fingertips, squeezing her tightly again, his heart pounding and booming in his chest, his temples now pulsing with raw desire. Only when he saw her eyes shut, as if wanting to be kissed, did he take a step back and walk away, letting out his breath in quick puffs. Patience, he said to himself. The next time I'll give her the full treatment: 'you might as well know this, Annie: when I am awake I think of you, and when I sleep I dream of you.' Certainly innocuous babble, but she'll eat it up. What is it about Annie? What mysterious factor gives her that lovely halo that makes her glow with strange sensuality? She's not a perfect beauty for sure, and when she laughs, I see only one dimple, and her forehead is round and ample—perhaps a trifle too ample.

On the way down to the plant offices, Dr. Bates beeped Victor Feng and then he called Phil Kerdes at the corporate offices. He hoped Phil would make sure that Alex Panagora had his calendar free for Thursday morning, at 11:00 a.m. Alex is so aggressive, and

Phil's so loyal that he's almost accusing Alex of father's murder; it all seems like a plain case of jealousy. It is possible, but Phil never mentioned he himself wants to be president of Bates Pharmaceuticals. He called Cecilia Van Osburgh and agreed to call her again in the morning to confirm lunch.

But just as he was leaving the Plant, Pia—also called by her close friends LaMía Pia—darted out of the Cost Accounting section and cut in front of him.

"I got to tell you something, Ivon."

"Yes, Pia?"

"Something fishy is going on around here, Ivon. I keep hearing Melissa panting, moaning, and talking to herself in her office. No, no, it's more like babbling, like she was speaking in tongues, but I know she's no Pentecostal. I've mentioned this to Tom, but he only tells me to hush…that I'm imagining things. My woman's intuition tells me something strange is going on, but I can't go back there because it's a restricted area and you know I would never break the rules. But it's all so strange, Ivon. I wish you'd give me permission to go in there to check it out."

"Maybe she's a shaker, holy roller, or charismatic?"

"A heathen committing whoredom and fornication. That's what she is!"

She nervously hitched up her undergarments and snapped the elastic band at her waist. "But the Domine doesn't discriminate against them, for he said, 'Be still and know that I am God: I will be exalted among the heathen. I will be exalted in the earth.'"

"Don't you worry, Pia, I'll look into it."

He headed toward the front gates where Victor was parked. She means well, Pia, but she gets so excited that her overbite seems even bigger. She seems like a fine God-fearing woman or perhaps a fiend-fearing woman, but what could make her think Melissa La Monalisa—for that's what the Hispanic workers call her—talks to herself; maybe it's the other way around? But for her to say that she hears her panting and moaning and committing whoredom? Ah, the mysteries of the human soul. Till then sit still, my soul. The grand aisle seemed even grander to him at the moment. He glimpsed the sun slanting through the stained-glass windows by the archway and he thought how wise his father had been in buying this old Plant. Outside, just before he got into the limo, he saw the half-barrel vaults, the load-bearing walls, the slender turrets, and he nodded in approval.

*Be still and know that I am God*, he repeated inwardly. Why is it that this brief word points to the soul, with knowing, and with God? *Still. Still. Still.* I bet Cecilia knows about this, what part of speech it is and its functions; after all, she's an expert in Professor Chomsky's generative grammar. *'Still still still'* echoed in his mind like an obstinate musical tune that annoys to no end until we whistle it out.

And why am I pondering this imponderable? Yes, it is all because of Pia's babbling.

Cecilia will know what this little word means; of course, she does: didn't she use this same word at the Chamber Music Society concert? Yes, of course, she said those melancholy silences were still points. Language is the bridge to the divine. These thoughts made him feel close to the divine, attuned to the universe, and that nothing was beyond his grasp—making him think that the blow to the head was responsible. With that surge of faith and confidence—in his ability to interpret, analyze, and synthesize data—he said to himself, "I will ask Phil again about the cash flow statement, I will ask him to explain the figures once again, and I am sure this time I will get it."

# Chapter 18 — A Plan for Hog

"How are things at Bates Pharmaceuticals, you Bates fat cats?" asked Hog, who had been waiting for them at the recently renovated Roy Roger's on Bergenline Avenue and 47th Street. The fake fireplace along with new furniture and décor, made the place feel warm and cozy, in contrast to the hostile artic blasts that were sweeping across Hudson County.

"Cool, Hog. No problemo, just tons of work," said Cowboy.

"Could you treat me to an apple pie, Cowboy? I need a bit of sugar."

"Sure, Hog. Anything you want, my man—just keep in mind that sugar is the enemy."

Hearing this—and much to his delight—Hog went for the 16-piece chicken tenders, a large order of fries, a salad, and "Fix me a vanilla milkshake, okay, pal?" And he swallowed his pride and the enormous meal.

Cowboy said, "If Lou's still pissed because of Dion Loco Bromius, you can stay in my house in Bogota—that cough sounds bad, man." He handed him a sheet of paper with his address in Bogota.

"And here's a bottle of cough syrup," said Lenox Jr. "Joey tells me you been sleeping here and there, on doorways. You could catch pneumonia, man. I live in West New York, closer than Joey's place, if you don't mind us poor black folks."

"Thanks, Lenox. For now, I'm sleeping in Satendar's store. Satendar is my Indian friend, or maybe he is Pakistani. I got bad news, guys: Dion Loco Bromius is now running around with Donato Sabellius, the Vampire! Donato is the high priest of a vampire church now, but I remember seeing him around since we were kids. He's about my age. I only see him at night—never during the day! Dude moves in the dark like a ghost."

Having finished his meal, Hog continued. "I hear Dion is saying he'll never forgive you for taking Lisa away from him and for shooting his ear off the other night. Bad news, man, he's swearing up and down that Lisa, Ariana, and others connected with Bates are fair game too. Also, Coz is making threats about Bates Pharmaceuticals; you know he's a Union organizer and a mean, sneaky dude. What happened at the Napalm Alley, anyway? World

War Three? I hear Donato is claiming the Bates Plant is his property and that he will punish not only Ivon Bates but his girlfriend, too—he's been showing a picture that he's cut out from a newspaper. Says anyone who sides with the Bates family are his enemies."

"Now I get it, the sideburns!" exclaimed Cowboy. "These two bums, Dion and Coz, smashed the vans at the plant! Keep you ear and nose to the ground, Hog. If you see or hear anything suspicious, you call me. I am afraid something is going down." As Joey and Lenox strode to their van, Cowboy felt eyes watching him, his rat-tail stiffening, and a chill running down his spine. What was that? He thought he'd seen two caped silhouettes draw into the alley. "You see anything, Lenox?"

"Yeah, two dudes, like Batman and Robin—weird, man."

"That man Donato—dude that looks like one of them smooth preachers on TV—and Dion Loco Bromius, his closest disciple, are messing with my mind. These nitwits are no plain folks, but two crazy fanatics, two screwballs, and they have many followers—the Sabellians. Damn creeps are up to something! Something bad is gonna happen, Lenox. We should tell Tom Stone that they were talking about Ivon's girlfriend."

# Chapter 19 — Phil O. Kerdes, Controller

On Thursday, December 21st, Ivon got to the office before the staff. Although his mind was teeming with optimistic projects and plans, dark thoughts oppressed him and made him feel vulnerable. The attack at that night-club, the ominous threat in the note slipped under his door, the union problems at the plant, Alex Panagora's demands for ownership in the company, the loan looming large and eroding his mind, the cash flow drying up, Annie Norris constantly asking about co-ownership of the patent; and on top of it all, Tom Stone warning him about the Sabellians' threat against Laura—all these things flooded his mind with anxiety, with somber foreboding, crowding him into a zone of dementia.

How do you shake this sense of vulnerability?

We need cash!

He was anxious that Stuart Potter at Manufacturers was taking his sweet time, dragging his feet with that damn loan. A gentle rap on the door drew him out of his mental chattering, and a second later, Phil O. Kerdes walked in. Ivon smiled and rose. "Listen, Phil: before I forget to tell you…Annie Norris is in the throes of a breakthrough at the Plant, and you can be sure that research is about to pay out. You know anything about Dad promising to let Annie co-own half of the patent?"

"Nope. Ready for your meeting with Alex?"

"Today, I only want to do a little fact finding with Alex."

"Just remember, Ivon, don't let him walk all over you. Don't give him an inch. Stand firm—you're the boss, Ivon." Phil ambled to the door, turned around and asked, "Any word from Manufacturers about the loan yet?"

"Nothing yet." Ivon watched Phil go out the door, shaking his head in disgust. He wondered if he hadn't erred miserably in overriding Phil's cautious advice. What had come over him to ignore Phil's experience and intelligence, too? Father was fond of saying, "When Old Phil thinks you can almost see his synapses light up!"

Knowing that Phil was a little touchy and irritable lately, he attributed that to the death of his wife Faye last year. Poor Phil! Faye had died from ovarian cancer and the medical plan had not covered all the expenses, making him bitter. That he now had to look after his two daughters all by himself did not help matters. Perhaps it's high time for Bates Pharmaceuticals to lighten his burden and pick up some of those bills—if not all of them. It's only fair. Yes, he resolved, once the cash from the Manufacturers' loan comes in, Bates Pharmaceuticals will pay those onerous bills and perhaps even set up scholarships for his two daughters. Too bad Columbia University rejected them; unless the girls got scholarships, Phil would have had a tough time paying that exorbitant tuition.

Ivon called Cecilia Van Osburgh, who agreed to meet him for lunch at 2:00 p.m. at Domenico's. Next, Ivon called Laura Standish, and she agreed to dinner on Friday evening. A vague sense of guilt, frustration, and remorse swept through him: guilt from knowing he was wooing Laura while he still thought of Cassandra, frustration because Cecilia disliked Laura so vehemently and he'd never act in such a way as to aggravate Cecilia. And remorse because he'd been toying in a vile manner with that lovely innocent soul, Annie Norris. Oh, Cassandra, Cass, Cassie, fire of my loins…Laura, Lor, Lo, unmatched in build and beauty, so feminine! He saw Laura gauze-gowned, sandaled, hair flowing, a bright, teasing smile, fleeing—always fleeing—through green meadows.

What if she only wants the Bates account?

What if she's only after a fat fee for taking the company public?

After all, she is a broker-dealer or a market maker; say it isn't for fees, Laura! So, what if she wants to make money? And what is wrong with that, and why not? Ah! But she could be worse than Cassandra. *You will lose…the laurel, the trunk, the plant, and the offshoots: an evil seed and a good seed.* And Annie Norris, too, wants something—that patent business. Do Americans live in a society that forces them to extract something from each other? A wave of despair washed down his back as he stood struggling not to succumb to another bout of depression. "Even if I feel this inward malaise, this inward dread, I must not show it. Wear a mask, hood yourself, Ivon! Pretend a cowl hangs over your mien." Stilled by doubt and lack of will, he forced himself to go around his office, pacing at a nervous clip, replaying in his mind Laura's sweet voice: "Ivon Bates is that you?" Oh—Laura! To hear her voice…sweet agony…is to hear the music of the stars. Even the mere sounds—

Laura, Lor, Lo, love—put him in a blissful but guarded state.

"I must protect her! Even if I get another blow to the head," he vowed.

While he waited for Alex Panagora, he outlined a lecture he had agreed to deliver at the Fashion Institute of Technology in the upcoming spring semester. Brian Dedrick, a Yalie friend—a fraternity brother, too—and now a young assistant professor of Marketing at FIT, had persuaded him to talk about new trends in the global economy. Brian Dedrick, better known at Andover and Yale as 'Beedee,' short for brain dead. "Sure, Beedee," Ivon had replied, "no sweat. I'll do it since I have some good ideas about that topic. But since you know Stewart Potter at Manufacturers better than I do, how about a *quid pro quo* — could you ask him to speed up that five million dollar loan?"

As he put his notes away, he fancied The FDA would surely grant the patent for Annie's new drug. The licensing of the Bates patents—new and old — to foreign corporations could well earn a good 50 million in royalties from the Asian market alone. "So why begrudge Annie Norris' wish to co-own the patent? A man has to have a sense of fair play, a sense of justice," he mused.

But not so amusing was the thought that Stuart Potter was dragging his feet. Now suppose the loan doesn't go through—what would happen? Disaster! He gasped. All that equipment it's on its way and Phil won't be able to pay bills. He's pushing all the accounts payable to net-45 as it is.

"I'm facing a financial melt- down!" he exclaimed.

Unable to come up with any creative solutions, he felt a thrill of fear, a cold tingle of terror running through his spine, lodging in his throat, strangling him as if a frozen severed hand—gangrenous green—was choking him. He could just hear Phil's blaming, harsh words. "I told you to wait, Ivon. I told you to order that equipment after you got the loan. It is your fault! You put us in a bind; your father would never have done this! I spent my whole life helping your father build this company and now I have nothing—not a pot to piss in!"

He strode to the window and peered outside. To feel better, he thought of Cecilia—his perennial tower of strength, his rock of Gibraltar—Van Osburgh. But as he cracked the window, he glimpsed some homeless women outside, prompting him to call

Phil on the intercom, asking him to pledge an annual gift to the hot lunch program fund run by The Church of St. Paul. Yes, Phil, right across from Fordham University, on 64th Street. Everyone should have a right to eat a hot meal in this great country.

When he returned to close the window, he saw the sun was out, but slow-moving dark clouds covered it. Ah, such is the power of errant cloud that can take away the splendor of the day. It's time for that meeting with Alex Panagora, the thick-skinned and aggressive Director of Marketing, Sales, and Public Relations.

Alex Panagora knocked on Ivon's door with such force that it made Ivon jump an inch off his seat. It was 11:10 a.m. when Alex came into Ivon's office, but only for a second, for he quickly said, "I'll be back in five minutes, Ivon. I have to get some mints." Ivon shrugged and went back to his notes. Shortly before 11:30, Alex returned, and walking right in, he sat down on the couch. Rattling a plastic container of orange-colored mints, he asked Ivon, "Want some?"

Ivon shook his head. "No, thanks."

Coming around his desk, Ivon sat down next to Alex, his back against the corner of the couch. Alex was a six-footer, stocky, with heavy thighs and round hips and bottom. His face was clean-shaven, except for the Hitler mustache; Ivon could smell traces of an expensive man's cologne. Strong scent! Having paid little attention to Alex in the past, he now observed his features, ticks, and mannerisms. Hmm, that expensive silk tie, pudgy hands with manicured fingers, graying hair fastidiously combed over to hide a freckled baldpate.

"I've been meaning to meet with you, Alex," Ivon said softly, "but it's been so busy tying up so many loose ends, things my father left undone. I apologize."

Alex nodded. "*Apologee 'cepted.*"

The strange accent made Ivon wonder how an Australian-Greek could ever end up working at Bates Pharmaceuticals. "Today, I just want to ask you a few basic questions. So, let's leave any major points for the New Year; I'm planning to spend more time here next year and we can then meet more often."

Alex was all business. "I have a lot of *oideas* and plans of me own for this *companee* and I think you should be interested in listening. Splendid *oideas* indeed. But as you said, let's leave them for January. *How'evah,* I have a couple of points I want to *moike* to *ye* so that ye can start thinking about them."

"I'm listening."

Then Alex reached for his shirt pocket and brought out a pack of dark, thin Turkish cigars. He tapped one out and lit it.

"Alex, please don't."

"All right, Ivon, I *apolojoize*! I forgot *yer* a bit delicate."

Both were careful not to offend each other, but Ivon couldn't help recalling some of the nasty rumors and hearsay that Ketty had passed on to him about Alex. Alex seemed ill at ease now, reporting to a young man who only a few years back had been but a pimply kid! "I want *ye* to know, Ivon," Alex said, choosing his words carefully, "that me *contreebushan* to this *companee* has been *'nowmas*. No one *besoides yer* fawther is more *responseebel* for the growth than me, and I you should act *'cordinglee*."

"Go on."

Alex smiled coldly. "*Compensashan* is *foin*, but I have other concerns, Ivon: I mean ownership as *recognishan* for a *shuperior* performance. I'd like to be *recognoized* for me *administroitive* skills, too. I will present ye with a memo *detoiling* some *oideas* about *reorgaeezashan* and *aconomees* for the *companee*."

"I welcome your ideas."

Noticing that Alex's shoulders had taken on a stance of dark disdain, eyes glistening with resentment, Ivon said, "We're going to explore a broad-based stock ownership for everyone, Alex."

"It doesn't have to be broad, and *certoinly* not for everyone, Ivon," Alex growled. "I'll be happy if *ye* count me, Tom Stone and Sabino at the plant, Phil here, and a few senior lab people you may want to include. No need to include all the grease balls. *Ye* have these Puerto Ricans, Blacks, Mexicans—these darkies, goddamned looting savages who should be mowed down with machine guns and erased from this world…"

"And you'd mow down Tom Stone, too?"

"Well, errrr, not him—he's decent…doesn't act like the rest of them." Listening to those alien words, an inexpressible sadness and pity settled in Ivon's heart. Having heard rumors about Alex's bigotry and hatred was one thing, but to listen and experience that directly was a shock to him.

Mowed down?

Are we harboring a Neo-Nazi here?

How can anyone have such a warped view of people? Such insensitivity! Ketty had warned him that Alex was an avowed racist, but he had refused to believe it. Let's be prudent. These thoughts depressed him so much that he wished he could go home, curl up in his bed, and so suspend the absurdities of a cruel world.

"Let's meet again first week in January, but please don't insult people, okay?" Having said this, Ivon felt a great sense of relief. No sooner had Alex left than he rushed to his desk where he found some paper napkins to wipe his hands off. But something was still gnawing at the edge of his mind. What is it? Suddenly a thought came to his mind, and he dashed to the door and saw Alex in Phil's office. He shouted:

"Alex, could you come back for a minute?"

"Forgot something, Ivon?"

"One final point. This may seem like something petty on my part, but I think the opposite. The next time we have an appointment, please keep the appointments for the time set. I would never consider keeping you waiting for twenty minutes—or any length of time."

"Well, Ivon…I'm a *buse*e person. I can't stick to the a*zact* minute."

"Look, Alex…We had an appointment for eleven o'clock this morning. You waltzed in ten minutes late, and then you turned around and disappeared for another twenty minutes."

"Surely, *ye*…"

Ivon interrupted Alex. "Let me finish. From now on, I will hold you to the exact minute whenever you and I have an appointment. It's very simple; if you're late one minute, there'll be no meeting. Is that clear?"

Watching Alex's face glow with a murderous blazed in his eyes, he thought, Is it possible he's capable of murder? Detective Wilkins thinks so, and Phil Kerdes comes just short of accusing him openly. They stared at each other in stony silence and for what seemed an eternity. But since Ivon wasn't about to break the silence—being fully aware that he had asked Alex a question, he waited for the answer—Alex finally relented. "Righto, Ivon," he said with reluctant acquiescence, "I'll be on *toim*." He minced away with his nose high in the air.

With his hands trembling and his mind obfuscated, Ivon rushed to the bathroom, where he scrubbed his hands thoroughly. As he dried his hands, he felt the pent up negative feelings and tension fade, and he now looked forward to having lunch with Cecilia Van Osburgh.

# Chapter 20 — Taking a fall

The intercom on Camilla's desk crackled with Helen McCain's harsh voice. "Camilla, please get me Randall Dodge at Empire HMOs. If he's out, keep trying. It's important." A few minutes later, Camilla's voice came over the intercom. "Mr. Dodge's secretary says he'll be in meetings all morning, but he will call you after lunch. Are you all right, Helen? Looks like you took a fall."

"I stepped into a puddle this morning. As soon as Randy Dodge calls, I'm going home."

Seeing her boss so distraught, Camilla sat next to her and touched her hand. "Let me play your favorite piece," said Camilla. "Rachmaninoff's Rhapsody on a Theme of Paganini, which always seems to soothe you."

Striding to the wall unit—a hand-finished cherry veneer set—Camilla turned on the stereo, and a moment later the melody filled the office. Within seconds, McCain felt better. Amid so many contretemps, music finds a way to reward a longing soul. Ah, yes. Rhythm. Everything—music, the body of a woman, the menses, blood, poetry, Henry Moore, Georgia O'Keefe, the heart, the pulse—everything is rhythm.

In a while, Camilla returned with a notepad. "What about the taping for PBS? And what do we do with Mr. Watanabe, Mr. Kimura, and Mr. Tachikawa? And shall I call Carol? No sense in her coming if you're fatigued."

"Cancel the taping thing! And tell Carol not to come today; tell her we'll still pay her two hours. If I feel better, I'll exercise with the barbells at home. Next, call the three samurais: Tofu, Tojo, and Mojo, and reschedule them. Just make sure you apologize profusely. You can tell them I'm ill, but smile and bow, pull your gums back and show teeth when you talk to them—they go for that gummy, toothy crap. Japs are ceremonious yet dangerous, that's why we couldn't trust them during the Second World War and locked their bony asses in concentration camps. Why can't these people shake hands or hug or embrace like most Christians? Well, at least they don't go around kissing air—*muah muaaah*!—like those onion-munching cheese farting French."

"Sure, no problem, Helen. I'll make the calls and will handle

Tofu, Tojo, and Ohio," replied Camilla with a wide, toothy, gummy grin while backing away with quick tiny steps and mocking bows, mimicking a geisha.

"Also, fix an agenda for the Executive Committee meeting, make a list—take this down." With both clarity of thought and speech, she rattled off the topics, Camilla struggling to keep up with her.

1. Sales Settlement with the Justice Department.

2. Write off of Novatol-6.

3. Sale or Lease of Patents for Marginal Products.

4. New Position: Eastern Europe Director.

5. Swap REITS for Treasury Stock.

6. Buyout of Bates Pharmaceuticals.

7. Open More Limited Partnerships.

Barely had Camilla stepped out the door when McCain twirled around her desk, swooning, following the piano and the strings. Love that Rushky Rachmaninoff!

In the afternoon, Randall D. Dodge returned McCain's telephone call. After a few amenities, McCain got straight to the point. "Randall, you really dropped a bombshell on me. Taking Orbis off the 'formulary' is a terrible step." McCain knew the crippling impact that could bring to a pharmaceutical company by excluding it from an HMO's formularies. Since the HMO doctors prescribed only products listed on the formularies, the excluded company's sales would suffer. Close to 60 million Americans are now covered under managed care with skimpy prescription plans.

"We asked you for rebates and discounts and you did not budge even for a paltry one percent. A lowly one percent! Bates Pharmaceuticals complied with everything we asked," said Randall Dodge.

"What can we do?"

"Too late now."

As the line went dead, she thought: Goddamned faggot communist! So enraged she became that had this been a face-to-face meeting, nothing could have prevented her from smacking that odious little man. How in the hell can Bates comply? They must be 'dumping' just like those hateful Japs do with microchips. Selling below cost! It's high time to hit Bates Pharmaceuticals!

"Ivon Bates," she lisped. "You might have a Ph.D., but I have my IUD. First the father got in the way, and now the son, but soon to be an unholy ghost."

Tormented and scarred by hurtful memories, she sighed with resignation, "It is my ill fate to have been a husbandless woman, destined to suffer a tortured hellish life. The mere mention of the Bates name repulses me, fills me with a poison whose only antidote is death. If it wasn't because of Sabino Yamamoto's threat…telling me I would swallow mud in this life and eternity…and I had to pay attention to that man, a man not given to idle threats."

This is not a fatal cosmic event! Ivon Bates, you're just a kid, sonny boy. After all, Orbis has a fine track record: five horizontal mergers, seven takeovers—of which five were hostile—and five outright buyouts of distressed companies. On her way out, Helen McCain stopped by Henry the Eight's office. Yes, Henry had hired Susan Connelly as a troubleshooter—a management trainee.

"Hire that Alex Panagora away from Bates immediately. Maybe he can persuade Randy Dodge."

Just then, Susan Connelly walked in to drop a file on Henry's desk.

Damn you Henry the Eight and your inches! McCain thought. Great teeth, elegant, wears that expensive suit with as much ease as he wears that lustful yet stiff smile. Don't you become a victim like Henry the Eighth's wives: one—Anne Boleyn, born with six fingers—beheaded, and the other, Catherine of Aragon, sister of Juana La Loca—more loco than a goat. Heh, Heh, Heh.

Stomping off, with her shoes clacking as if they were backless or two sizes too large, she puttered under her breath, "Oh, King Henry the Eight; what good are looks without brains? Your shoes are full of fecal matter. Heh, heh, heh. I know what has to be done. Just leave matters to the *uberfrau*!"

# Chapter 21 — Ivon Bates, Ivy Star

Cecilia was sipping a cocktail when Ivon arrived at Domenico's. Not missing the clue from Walter, the Maitre d', the attentive waiter promptly and with great alacrity took their orders, Cecilia ordering the Cacciucco—her favorite fish soup—and Ivon the red snapper. Having noticed that she kept fidgeting with her napkin, Ivon let her take the initiative.

"Ivon, I need your opinion," Cecilia whispered. "You know I'm on the Met's Board, and on April 30th, Christie will action two of my favorite masterpieces. The first piece is Gauguin's Still Life with Hope and the second one is Van Gogh's Interior of a Restaurant."

Ivon felt a jolt, and he thought, "There is that *still* word again: Still Life with Hope. What a pithy and yet glorious title for a painting! Not only was Gauguin a painter but also a poet who could divine such a link: still life and hope, immobility and expectancy, motionless life in some future. His mind traversed time and space to his childhood, and it was as if he could feel Cecilia steering him through the different bays and galleries at the Metropolitan Museum of Art and the Museum of Modern Art. Degas' bright loud watercolors flashed in front of him, and next Van Gogh's Starry Night.

"That Van Gogh may be worth at least five million dollars!"

Cecilia said, waving a thick glossy brochure, "Ten. I'm thinking of putting in a bid."

"Tell me about the title Still Life with Hope; it seems such an odd juxtaposition."

"Yes, Ivon. In fact, I have a personal theory that what makes an artist a great artist is this same point: a great artist must own a grasp of creation, of infinity, and of the sublime. If these qualities lack in a work, then the artist will remain at the fringes of greatness."

"So, you see a connection to the sublime in this painting?"

"Oh, yes, indeed! Hope at the end of life, and hope after still life, is the most exquisite exploration of the divine. But that is a grand theme for a doctoral dissertation, a topic I've discussed a few times with Eddy Said at Columbia. In fact, Edward is coming to my New Year's party. You'll meet him then and you'll have a chance to explore this topic in greater depth."

"Now I am looking forward to it. Laura is also excited but quite nervous about your party. She's got this funny idea that she'll feel out of place with all those distinguished professors."

"Oh, no need for that, for I'll have an eclectic group. We'll have fun—you'll see. And I'll have a chance to converse with Laura. So far, I am very impressed by her voice, that Boston accent with a trace of what may be a pretentious British accent, that throaty languorous quality. But all that is trivial. I am interested in her ideas, her cultural taste. I hate to see you waste your time with a bubble-headed beauty who doesn't have the faintest idea who Lacan, Garcia Marquez, Alan Greenspan, Santiago Calatrava, I.M. Pei, or the Dalai Lama might be."

Ivon returned to the art topic. "I gather then that you want to buy art."

"I have an accumulation of Blue-Chip stocks, triple A grade corporate bonds, municipals bonds, and mutual funds. I would like to buy the Van Gogh and donate it to the Museum in memory of your father and me. In that way, the Bates name and mine will survive in perpetuity."

Ivon raised his brows. "That's a lofty thought, Cecilia, and I thank you for that. I say go ahead; it seems you can afford it."

"The market's been generous. Besides, since I own my pied-à-terre on Sutton Place Square, I feel very secure."

"With four bedrooms and a formal dining room, I wouldn't call it that."

"Well, it seems so small lately. Antonia has now moved in and taken over one of the large bedrooms; she didn't want to live alone after Lola moved into one of the NYU dorms. Also, your old bedroom is now my library.

Pressed as he was for cash, for an instant Ivon thought if Cecilia would be receptive to making a cash loan to the Company, and he would have asked her right then had she not exclaimed,

"It's settled! Come April, I'll go ahead, unless I find a better cause."

Judging that Cecilia was now in a good mood, he once again mentioned Laura Standish, for he wasn't sure whether he had detected a bit of hostility earlier. So now he wasn't surprised by Cecilia's opinion:

"She has that old-guard chic look and a self-assured manner, but I sense you might get hurt if you get involved with her. She seems to be an ambitious, driven young woman, saving herself for old wealth, and she should be since she comes from the poor branch of that family. I've made some inquiries. She lives with her aunt in a one-bedroom apartment at Central Park South, and half of her salary goes to pay for her student loans. She is wealthy in pedigree but student-loan poor—the dear soul."

So much for the IRS—the immensely rich set—thought Ivon.

"Enjoy life, my dear. You're much too young for commitments or some ill-fated mésalliance."

Changing the subject, Ivon mentioned his problems with Alex Panagora. Cecilia scowled. "That horrible man! You can't trust that man, Ivon. You know he wants shares in the company and to be the president of Bates Pharmaceuticals."

"How do you know about his intentions?"

"This past summer he demanded to see me," Cecilia's voice trailed. "I acceded, and we met for lunch. Such a vulgar person! He told me that since you were so inexperienced and way too young, he should run the company. I just don't like that man. And that awful accent that he willfully flaunts is offensive. To paraphrase Hamlet, 'The serpent that did sting thy father's life, his crown wants to wear.' Phil Kerdes is sure he killed your father—or if he didn't do it himself, at least he's an accomplice—and I am now inclined to believe Phil. I love Phil as much as I despise Alex."

"I'll ask him not to pester you again."

"That advertising agency on the sixth floor might move out soon, and if that happens, I'm planning to lease the entire sixth floor. I need you to design and to decorate a boardroom, a combined reception room, library, and directors' conference room. What do you think? And this is just the beginning, because if I take the company public I will build an administrative building right next to the Plant."

"I'm so happy to see you in full charge of the company, so level-headed, and so different from the hot-headed forward who played for the Yale Bulldogs. You're a gentleman now, not a hot-headed Friars and Monks pledge anymore."

"Cecilia, I've been in one fight, and that was when I was a sophomore."

"Ivon, are you forgetting that nasty game at Levien gymnasium with the Columbia Lions right here in the City? It was your senior year!"

"What! You were there? You never told me this."

As if sharing a secret, she lowered her voice, "Well, your father asked me to promise not to tell you he had been there to see you. He was such an eccentric about showing a soft side, but when that Columbia substitute came running from the bench and sucker-punched you, I had to contain Joe. And if Ted, the provost, hadn't held him back, he would have dashed out the door. We watched the game and sipped martinis from the VIP lounge."

"My father!"

He felt like kissing and hugging Cecilia and he wanted to cry out loud, but he kept his composure. Who knew the old man had an ounce of feeling about anybody other that himself.

Cecilia's eyes lit up. "You played well that night, Ivon."

"I don't know why, but that year there was bad blood between Yale and Columbia. Three seconds to go and the score was 80 to 79. Columbia ahead. The point guard threw me a blind pass. I could never understand how he knew where I was unless he had eyes on the back of his head—but he knew! I slam-dunked that sucker so hard I had to hang on to the ring. I was afraid I would get a technical because I dangled there for an eternity, but the official let it go and we won!"

A strange yearning filled his heart. You are my proper mother, Cecilia. But resigned to not knowing his biological mother, he thought: Maybe one day I will. But till then I'm happy to have you as my mother, and Antonia as my second mother—my *mama*.

"By the way, you keep in touch with any Friars and Monks?"

"Oh, yes, with some. My friend 'Beedee' teaches at the Fashion Institute of Technology; he is a Friar. Laura tells me she is in touch with a few Friars and Monks who are doing well in investment banking. Stewart Potter and two others are in commercial banking. I also see Fred Morse, who is a bartender at Toros y Cuernos on Second Avenue, where I go for a few beers once in a while."

"To meet girls, you mean," said Cecilia with a twinkle in

her eyes that declared, I know about those meat bazaars. "What's the difference between Friars and Monks?"

Ivon grinned. "C'mon, Cecilia, you know I can't divulge that. Right after I put on my tunic and pulled the cowl over my head, *L'Abbe Noire* said, "If any man has an ear, let him hear—but not from thee." Ivon sighed and looked at her with tenderness. Yet, certain shredded, unwanted memories of Cecilia's fiery and complex character surfaced: *Twins, for heaven's sake! Your seed, you monster! Even the most vicious beasts care.*

Just before they reached the front foyer, the Maitre d' called, waving a booklet, "Ms. Van Osburgh, you forgot your brochure. Such lovely colors!"

"Keep it, Mr. Benjamin, and look at it. It's a fine example of a work of art in the age of mechanical reproduction." To Ivon, she whispered, "We shall own the original."

With a hug and kiss, they parted. Having felt for so many years so unwanted and so unloved by his father, Cecilia's revelation about his father's soft side filled him now with warm bliss.

"Father loved me!" he exclaimed, wishing with all his soul to believe it.

# Chapter 22 — A Blood Bonus

For three days Helen nursed a cold, returning to the office on Thursday to wish the staff a joyous holiday and to talk to Chief Lester Lowmax. Afterward, she planned to go to F.A.O. Schwarz to get some toys for her nephews.

Move it, move it! She had to dodge several speeding cabs. Watch out for that cab, quick, quick, quick; he's driving like a madman. Only after she was safe on the sidewalk did she see the cab driver giving her the finger. Russians and Pakistanis are the worst cabdrivers! Tons of these people populate our lovely city now and not a single one who speaks acceptable English. They all speak gibberish and who knows what they plot—always conspiring on their two-way radios and cell phones, casting furtive glances, their scabrous, slit pig eyes dancing with distrust and malice, full of seditious thoughts, full of treachery, yet empty of respect for the land that keeps them fed, fat and fetid. Shoes in fecal matter!

As soon as she reached the office, McCain asked Camilla to call Lester Lowmax and tell him she would stop by his office at eleven thirty on her way out. When she stepped into the Panopticon, she recognized Freddy Morales and Zach Beasley, who were watching the rookie Orlando—Danny—Finzicontini operate on the console. Fixing her eyes on Morales first and then on Beasley, she thought, Oh, yes, here's the odd couple: Freddy Kruger-Rican and Zach of Shit, Gorilla and Guerrilla, or Cro-Magnon X and Neanderthal Y. Heh heh heh. Two monsters with barren souls.

"The Chief is expecting you, Ms. McCain," said Beasley as he closed the door.

The hushed talk—between McCain and Lowmax—had lasted less than five minutes; sufficient time for her to convey what she needed.

Helen concluded, "I will ride to the Bates Plant with you. I'm not the type of Commander-in-Chief who likes to stay on the sidelines."

"It's not my place to second guess you, Helen, but there's really no need for you to be in the field, being the CEO…things could go wrong…"

"That's exactly the point!" Helen's stare bored harshly into the Chief's eyes. "You allow wrong as a possibility—I don't!"

“No more thoughts and naked abstractions—it’s the time to act,” she muttered as she ambled to the elevators. “Lester, the Molester, must shit or get off the pot. Heh, heh, heh. What we’re going to do immediately after we buy them out is tear down that huge stupid sign in front of the building, a building that is a veritable old gothic structure! I wonder if there’s some truth to that legend that ghosts and vampires lived there. Now, were it not for Sabino doing all the dirty work for Joe Bates, Bates Pharmaceuticals would still be a low pesticide company. What about Santa Antonia? We’re surely underestimating how these immigrants are changing our once white America. These catholic South Americans are blunting—not that the other groups are blameless, they are the worst offenders—our sharp, cut-throat competitive Darwinian capitalism! God forbid one day they takeover; we’d a have a nation of soft namby-pamby yellow bellies.”

# Chapter 23 — Happy Holidays

On Friday morning, with everyone knowing that the following week the office would be closed, the Christmas spirit suffused the air in all the departments. But what thrilled everyone was the news that Ivon had told Phil the staff could leave by 1 p.m. Ivon went around the office wishing everyone a joyous holiday. When he stopped in Alex's Panagora's office, he made it a point to be friendly, and to show him he bore no ill feelings. Alex told Ivon that he had to see four odious doctors—*docktewrs*—four hot shots who were Rxing deluxe name drugs and not the Bates generics: "…'pon me honor, me boy, this will *choin*ge."

"Myrna, could you come in right away?"

As soon as Ivon left, Myrna returned. Alex said to her, "If the lad has any *broins* or street smarts, he will see that I am the only one who can *soive* the *campanee*. I'm sure he'll appoint me president of Bates Pharmaceuticals."

Her face shining with devotion, Myrna gushed, "Oh, Alex. Just thinking about that makes me so happy."

"This lad Ivon will run the *companee* into *bank'raptcy* if he *stois* as president. The dear chap is so green, so *noieef;* and all that *Oivee* League *ejucoishan* wasted. All those degrees for nothing! These Yank elite schools only teach blokes like Ivon useless liberal arts courses; they teach nothing of pragmatic *decishan* making required to *stoi aloive* in a tough world."

"You will be president, Alex!"

"Now, get me the addresses of these doctors," said Alex, slapping her bottom.

"Sure, Alex," Myrna said, and headed toward the door, swinging her wide hips. "But just in case I'm not here when you return, please look on top of your desk. I'll leave your Christmas present there. I would have given it to you now, but it's not going to be ready until two o'clock."

"What is it?"

"A surprise."

"C'mon Minnie, you pique me *cure-o-setee* then ye leave me dangling and inter'uptus." Alex pouted and plodded to the door where Myrna was standing and he touched her cheek.

Giving Alex a lucent gaze, Myrna said, "I love it when you

talk your Pig Latin." She then gazed around and seeing that they were alone she got close to Alex. Fixing his tie, she pushed her heavy bosom against Alex's chest, sliding her hand down his crotch and squeezing him hard.

"Wow, Alex, you've got to be proud of the family jewels you've got down under. You big handsome Aussie golden Greek—a *foin comboinashan.*" She mocked him jovially.

"You wicked *leetel divvle.*" Alex got aroused, but looked around as if afraid, his eyes betraying the thought. Someone could just walk in here! He felt Myrna jerk her pelvis backward and thrust it right against his groin. Holding on to her body, feeling her hips swaying gently and watching her eyes shut in glorious ecstasy, Alex breathed hard as he let her pelvis grind and rub up and down.

"You're so sweet, my Aussie hunk."

Their bodies welded as they stood still.

At last, Myrna detached herself and rasped, "Let me get that for you now. You'll find out what I got you in a couple of hours, and I'm sure you'll like it—I'll be back in a jiffy."

Five minutes later, Myrna handed Alex a sheet. "Here's the list you wanted. Oh, by the way, you had several calls from Mr. Henry Cook at Orbis Laboratories. He intimated that he might have good news—he actually used the word 'tidings'—for you. He really sounded very sweet, friendly, asking me to call him Henry—not Mr. Cook—right away. What's going on?"

"Well, ye know, he and Helen McCain want me. I'll be *deloighted* to tell ye everything after I meet with them. But not to *word*, ye and me are a team and if they want me, ye'll be in the *p'ck-ayge.*"

He left to see the odious doctors.

It was about 3 p.m. when he returned, and when he got off the elevator, he hustled to his office, eager to see Myrna's surprise gift, his eyes flashing with wild expectation. By Phil's desk, he saw a group—three clerks, Michael Lopez, Coral, Margaret Orr, and Ivon—drinking wine and engaged in animated conversation.

*Me present!*

Alex's eyes lit up as he zoomed on his desk. Picking up the slender tube, he bobbed it up and down in his right hand, guessing its content by the weight. What can it be? So well wrapped! Stiff, heavy old-gold Pergamum paper. He then undid the red bow, but clumsy with excitement, he tightened it even more, so he went around his desk and took out a pair of scissors, snipping off the damn bow at once.

Pulling the artifact out of the tube, he unwrapped it with trembling fingers. Look at this! It was an engraved bronze plaque set in a triangular, deep-stained, hand-rubbed mahogany piece of wood. Alex read it: *Alex Panagora, President*. What an exquisite piece of art! Such a noble handcrafted artifact! Yes, softer than a baby's bottom. Lifting the nameplate with both hands against the light, he held it there for some time as if he was trying to discern a fault. He seemed awed. The plaque glistened against the light, and as he brought it down to eye level, he kissed it gently, pressing it hard against his cheek. He turned on his desk lamp and studied the woodwork, rubbing the grains and pores under the warm glow of the lamp.

He then read the tiny card that was taped to the bow: Merry Christmas, A. P. Hail to the chief! Love, Myrna. Tiny hearts dotted the i's and the letter 'o' of love was a happy face.

Drawing a paper napkin from his coat pocket, he wiped off a few tears that had rolled down his cheeks and cleared his throat. Who else but Myrna would think of such a f*oin* gift? Such a *refoined* piece of *purpart*! He didn't feel the amber ball of spit dangling from his chin like a tiny spider swaying from its own thread. Only the plaque and the card counted. Pacing around his office, he moaned and mumbled,

"I am what I am, I *des'hve* to be president of the company and it's only fair since I brought all those monstrous accounts, accounts that are worth millions. Righto, old boy, monstrous they are."

Again, he lifted the plaque and kissed it.

Suddenly, he twirled around and he saw a man by his door. A deliveryman—a very short man, a Mexican—stood with a paper bag in his hand, a wet shabby apron dangling from his waist.

"Carnegie Curtain Deli," he announced, "did you order, sir?"

"No, I didn't order," said Alex in an angry tone, vexed by the intruding, impudent dwarf. "Let me see the goddamned slip."

Stepping close to the desk, the deliveryman showed him the green slip that was stapled to the bag. "This says fourth floor, we're on the fifth floor—you stupid fool!" Alex's eyes shone with mean harshness. "Learn English, you *imbeceel*!"

"*Hijo de la chingada, Chinga tu madre*," replied the man and when he reached the door he turned and repeated, "*Chinga tu madre chingao!*" running full-hilt into the elevator that was still on the floor.

Becoming rigid for a few seconds in his attempt to intuit what the man had said, Alex then lunged from behind his desk.

*Me mowther*!

Neither grace nor decorum lay in his mind as he ran—with clumsy camel steps—after the poor man, reaching the elevator just a second too late, the doors closing with a loud clang. "I'll call the *Immigro*ishan Department on you, you illegal alien wetback!"

As Alex trundled back to his office, he saw that Ivon, Phil, Michael, and two others in the group were staring at him. Waving, his Hitler mustache waggling, he shouted, "That bow-legged half-breed got *froish* with me! I *ashume* he insulted me *mowther in Mexican and that gibberish brings out the foighting speerit* in me—missed the lift by a bit."

Michael Lopez, CPA, the assistant controller, graduate of Hunter College, turned to Ivon and said, "I bet he didn't tip the poor man. Scrooge Panagora never tips the deliverymen more than a quarter. In his peculiar non-decimal system, a quarter is equivalent to fifteen percent for all his orders."

"Remember how he used to call himself 'Doctor Panagora' and had that printed on his business cards?" asked Michael Lopez.

Phil nodded. "Old Joe had to tell him that the fact he was a first-year medical school drop-out did not give him the right to be called doctor."

* * * *

That evening, Ivon and Brian Dedrick had dinner at Windows on the World at the Twin Towers. Afterwards, Victor drove them to Carmine's on the Upper West Side, where Ivon dismissed Victor for the night. They had a few drinks at the bar, but since the bar was thick with Columbia and Barnard undergrads, they left. They took a stroll south down Broadway, talking about the murder investigation. Then Ivon mentioned Laura Standish.

"Ah! So, you are the fortunate bastard."

"Well, nothing definite. That's why I want your advice."

"While the Brits have their princess Diana, we Americans have Laura—let me tell you, that's the closest we Americans we'll ever come to royalty. But I am a little surprised: I always thought she'd hold out for a fortune vaster and older than yours and for someone with good looks—and you're ugly. Just like Grace Kelly, who spurned all her Americans suitors and went for that dumpy little fat ass prince Rainier—you remember her? Imagine her going for a dumpy little guy whose entire country could fit inside Wollman Rink in Central Park. Some American women just can't get over the fact that we don't allow parasites and nobility in this country."

"Yeah, it's in the Constitution—right? The United States shall grant no title of nobility and no American citizen shall accept any title—something like that."

"The other night at a reception, I met this pretentious prune-faced twerp whose pompous husband introduced her to me as 'my wife, Lady Jane.' As I shook hands I said, 'jolly exceedingly pleased to make your acquaintance, and what would you like to have? I am the server here.'" Essaying a cynical smile, Beedee went on, "Anyway, what can Laura see in your ugly mug—which is uglier than my left armpit, not to mention my left testicle."

"Remember how she used to hang out with the IRS, Beedee?" It turns out she's all pedigree but no fortune. I got that from an excellent source. So, I am afraid she might have ulterior motives to use me to build her own fortune and then toss me for someone in her set. You might know I am thinking about signing her company to take Bates Pharmaceuticals public with an IPO. She's bound to earn a couple of cool mils."

"Wow! Just make sure you do all that 'Due Diligence' stuff. Make sure you aren't taken for a ride. Don't trust your own legal department—hire outside consultants to represent you. This is complicated stuff…those awful boring contracts, tombstones, prospectuses and so forth. If everything is okay, then go along with the flow, you creep," said Beedee jovially. "If white-armed Laura Standish is within your reach—go for it! I wouldn't mind parking my smelly boots under her bed. I'd let her use me, abuse me, reuse me, and then toss me and refuse me."

"Yea, well, that's you, Beedee. I don't want to be a pawn in her game."

"She's inscrutable. I grant you…could never figure her out. But, hey—she's the Homeric or Hellenic face that launched a thousand scholarships when she was a Yale undergraduate."

"You know Cass hung me out to dry, and it has taken me a long time to get over that."

"Oh, that Cass! Laura, though, is an Olympian grace or graces I should say, but guarded, sharp and clever. Watch it! A real combo of Cassandra, Calypso, Circe, Penelope—and maybe even Lesbos."

"Thank you for your false impressions, you dog breath! You just gave me some green hope—greener than your teeth. Anyway, you'll see Laura at Cecilia's New Year's party and you'll also meet some distinguished university professors from Columbia University. Of course, you'll make some connections yourself, Beedee. Since you want to spend your life in academia, why not in an Ivy League university?"

Changing the subject, Ivon said, "Detective Wilkins found a notation in dad's appointment book: 'ask Phil,' and right under that, a partial formula. He handed him a piece of paper which read: C = SN (d). We don't know what it means. Maybe you can find out."

"I think it's the first half of Black-Scholes-Merton's formula for valuing stock options. I'm almost sure. We had to learn that formula in graduate school. I'll check it out and then I'll call you or send you an E-mail."

Then, as if on a whim, Ivon asked Beedee if he knew anything about rocks, if he could distinguish them.

"Not really. What's on your mind?"

"Well, it's this tiny rock, spherical, that Sabino and I found in the swamp, next to the Plant. Sabino said it contains infinity."

"What? Didn't you study math, you dodo—duhhh! That whack to the head must have melted the wires in your brain. A set of infinite numbers contains itself and the infinite numbers, in theory. But something physical—like a rock or any tangible thing—can only contain itself and nothing else, let alone infinity; two things cannot occupy the same space. Sabino must have been teasing you, and I wouldn't doubt it, since you can be so naïve sometimes!"

They were standing at the corner of 80th Street and Broadway, in front of Zabar's, where Ivon flagged a cab and got in without even giving a glance to the two uniformed guards whose badges and insignias displayed the Orbis logo—Sergeant Morales and Captain Beasley—standing across the street.

# Chapter 24 — Ariana Naxos

Just before 2 p.m. on Sunday, Cowboy arrived in Guttenberg—Hudson Boulevard—to pick up Ariana at her home, a small house which faced east about fifty yards beyond the marina. As he looked around, he saw that Ariana's was the only house on the long block, standing there desolate like a tiny promontory on a deserted island. From the steps, he could see the eastern shore of the Hudson River and the Manhattan skyline.

They rode through the Lincoln Tunnel into Manhattan, to the Cats matinee at the Winter Garden Theater on 50th Street and Broadway. The tickets were Joey's Christmas present. During the intermission, he bought a colorful program, a T-shirt, and a poster for Ariana, who treasured the items as much as she did the ticket-stubs and two Stagebills that she had already stashed away. After the show, they strolled—holding hands—south to 42nd Street on the West Side of Broadway. The avenue—with the huge neon signs flashing and the store windows glittering with full Christmas décor—was teeming with pedestrians, thick and festive like a street fair: shoppers, tourists, sailors, 3-card Monte hustlers, concertgoers, peddlers, street musicians and other odd seekers. Ariana, being at her first Broadway show, appeared jittery about the grand musical she had just seen. She wore a dark blue dress with a red belt under her black winter coat and a black headband that had an embroidered wreath, which held her black hair back. Her hair was thick and fluffy and it streamed down her back, long strands curled in ringlets cascading over her shoulders, making her face look small, as if she was fearful.

Cowboy noticed Ariana didn't walk like most people, she walked with small flowing steps, and shoulders stiffly erect as if she was gliding, floating. Surely the prettiest girl here tonight, even without makeup! he thought. The darkness of her clothes and the flowing strands of her hair intensified the paleness of her face under the glowing lights of the bright signs and the opaque white-silvery moon. In front of the Marriott Marquis Hotel, at the corner of 45th Street, a mixed group of people clad in black stopped their chatter to stare at her, ignoring Cowboy as if he wasn't there. Suddenly three of them—three old women with deep shadows around their eyes, homeless in appearance—ran in front of them and drawing black-eyed Susan's, death lilies and white fern leaves from a basket, they sprinkled handfuls in front of Ariana.

"This is a weird group," thought Cowboy, "damn pranksters; like they just came out of their caskets and were out for kicks on a moonlit night." Gothic people? Vampires? Out of the corner of his eye, he saw that an even larger group was lurking in the shadows, wearing long black capes, aggressively baring their fangs, scratching the air, and hissing at him.

As if expecting trouble, Cowboy's eyes became harsh, his muscles tensing up. Ariana squeezed his hand, smiled, and with a calm voice said,

"Children will be children, even children of the nether world."

"Spooky freaks," he muttered.

Only after he saw she was unfazed by the vampires did he calm down. At 42nd Street, they crossed Broadway and returned to the East Side. From the garage Ariana gazed deep into Cowboy's eyes and said, "You help and free the frail. I felt you were ready to take on all those weird people and vampires to protect me."

"I'd put my life on the line for you, Ariana," said Cowboy. "I admire you, and with you by my side I don't feel so alone. You make me happy."

Removing her headband, Ariana gave it to him. "Here, Joey. Keep this. It has the thread of salvation, and every time you look at it, you'll think of me." She then kissed him gently.

"Wow, a magical headband? Sometimes I don't get you."

"A talisman for you! If you don't understand me sometimes, it's because I often say things I don't quite follow myself; I see images for which I have no words, images for which I have no life experience either. I live for love, poetry, and am always in search of the magical shore where neither pain nor suffering abide—only love."

"That's why you are a poet?"

"I love matching rhythm to images." Her eyes turned misty, dreamy, and childlike.

"You're so young and yet so wise, Ariana. It's a treat to talk with you because I learn things from you, not that I get everything you say, but when I'm with you, I don't feel so alone."

"Do you live with your parents?"

Cowboy held her long tapering fingers. "No, I live alone. My mother just passed away three months ago."

"I'm so sorry. Was she ill?"

"Yes. She was an alcoholic, and she drank herself to death—liver failure."

"Is your father still alive, Joey?"

"I think so, Ari. I think my father's still alive, but I don't know who he is. I never knew him. My mother was always very private about him, and she went to her grave taking the secret with her. It's such a mystery. The few times I asked her about my father or his family or other family, she'd start crying and would never speak about it. At times, I feel like I'm the son of a mad god or a criminal. I feel lost not knowing who I am, what my heritage is."

Ariana's voice filled with gentle tenderness. "I guess she was only trying to protect you, Joey," said Ariana; then she asked with deep interest, "Did she give you any hints or clues? Did you ask her how they met?"

"Yes, they met at Bates, that's all I know. I think some of the old-timers at the Plant know the story. But I'll find out, eventually."

Ariana's eyes filled with grief. "Just don't get too obsessed, Joey. You don't need your father's identity to make your own identity; you just don't manufacture a self from others, Joey. You are the I that acts not because of an inborn sense of self, but because you imagine yourself." In vain, he tried to find a simple meaning in her remarks. So, he let it go. They drove to Columbus Avenue, in the 80s, and had dinner in a Greek restaurant. When they got back to Guttenberg, it was close to 10 p.m., and shortly thereafter, Cowboy left Ariana's house. He walked back to his car and took off with a squeal of tires, but barely had he reached the corner when he slammed the brakes so hard that his head lurched forward against the windshield.

Icy stabs of foreboding pierced his heart.

He knew he had seen flitting shadows across Ariana's house by the marina. Backing up at full speed to the spot where he had seen the furtive silhouettes, he looked around. Nothing but gloom. As he heard screams tearing the glacial silence of the night, a restless tension built in his body. "Watching those gothic people and vampires has made me jumpy," he thought. More screams. Fear gripped his mind and for a brief fraction of time he faced the fact that perhaps he was physically ill or mad. "Oh God, don't let me be ill," he prayed as he floored the Impala away toward Bergenline Avenue.

# Chapter 25 — Cowboy at Headquarters

Melissa La Monalisa, Tom Stone's assistant, had called Ketty earlier to tell her that Dr. Bates was on his way and that Cowboy was driving the limo today, "Check him out, Ketty, but no monkey business, he is all mine!"

Sabino had asked Dr. Bates if he could keep Victor at the Plant to help him clear the drifts of snow that had blanketed the blacktop, the guard shack, the parking lot, and around the generator housing where the drifts reached 10 feet high. "A monstrous job, but Victor is so good with the snow blowers!"

"Of course, Sabino," Ivon said. "Joey can drive the limo. This is the greatest snowstorm the Northeast had seen in over 125 years—and there's no letup. One fine way to start the New Year! Do everything in your power to keep the Plant open."

When Dr. Bates stepped out of the elevator with Cowboy by his side, Ketty rushed to greet them. Dr. Bates removed his overcoat, shook it, and handed it to Ketty.

"What a mess!" Ketty exclaimed, and turning her attention to Joey, she said, "I've heard a lot about you, Joey De Lemos! I feel like I've known you for a long time, Joey—Mr. Cowboy."

"Hi, Ketty. Pia says you're an angel, and I agree. And let me tell you, Pia isn't a pushover."

Dr. Bates asked Ketty, "Is Phil in? Everything is such a mess out there at the Plant."

Ketty sighed, "Things aren't bad here in the city, and a small blizzard won't shut us down—everybody's in! That tells you about the quality of the staff."

Dr. Bates looked at Cowboy. "Come on in."

Ketty was about to head toward the Accounting section, to Michael Lopez's desk, when she saw Myrna and Patricia darting to her desk. "What a hunk!" Patricia exclaimed. "Looks like you two hit it off."

Ketty nodded. "Yeah, I like him a lot. He's so handsome and yet so masculine. He has a cleft chin!"

"I don't think he's that hot," Blow Hard Myrna smirked. "Nice bod, but I think he looks like a butcher's apprentice with that hideous haircut."

"Butcher's apprentice? More like a meat packer—packing a

fat Big Mac and two quarter pounders," said Patricia as she gave Ketty a malicious wink.

"Must you always be so vulgar, Pat? Then again, that's expected from someone who went to NYU!"

"Well, at least NYU doesn't produce tight-assed lesbians like Smith College."

"I went to Mount Holyoke! And don't you forget it!"

Then, seeing that Ketty was smirking and hardly containing a laugh, Myrna looked at her with fire in her eyes and said, "What are you smirking at? You never went to college—you went to a barnyard where they take rejects from Mount Holyoke, Vassar, and Radcliffe!"

Ketty hit back: "At least we at Barnard College don't major or go for ancient Australian and Greek fossils!"

Myrna blanched at the unmistakable allusion of her boss, Alex Panagora. "Uuuuuhhhhh…dizzzzzz…yo, man—in her face, major dizzzzzzz," titters of laughter howled from the small crowd now surrounding them.

Patricia giggled and guffawed openly.

Pointing a finger at Patricia, Myrna cackled, "Look who is laughing! You'd never get any kind of man with those flabby thighs, that heavy bottom, and droopy boobs."

Patricia—who was wearing an ankle-length flouncy skirt—lifted her skirt waist-high and twirled, showing her luscious thighs and indeed a heavy but firm bottom cleft by the thin string of a black thong.

"Have a look, girlie—no flab at all!"

She did an about face, bent a little, and wagged her practically bare plump rump at Myrna.

"Eat your heart out!" she said with an in-your-face sneer.

Speechless, Myrna trotted off in a huff, ignoring the catcalls, hoots, and jeers.

Slapping hands with Patricia, Ketty said, "You're way too cool, Trish. You did the impossible: you really shut her up—you really mooned her! For an instant, I was afraid you were going to turn about and show your Bikini Wax or unhook your bra."

No sooner had she said that than Alex Panagora, choking with anger, charged in. "Confound the place! What the hell's going on *heah*—I *preshume* you have the *die* off?" he demanded. "By

George, ye people would spend the whole die wagging yer tongues without doing a bit of work, making that lovely innocent child cry. The impudence! Things will *choinje* around *heah,* that I *promish*—and very *shoon*, too." He headed to his office, his round hips swiveling and quaking with his nervous trot.

"And it will be my honor to remember your mother, too," said Ketty in an undertone inaudible to the valiant Marketing Director.

Meanwhile, in his office, Dr. Bates asked Cowboy to put together a computer hutch and workstation. He told him that Marcus Feng was going to come in later to hook it up to the LAN. Just then, Phil walked in. When Dr. Bates introduced Cowboy to Phil, Phil zoomed through his thick glasses and his eyes seemed to discern in Cowboy's face a familiar likeness. The stunned look on Phil's face didn't go unnoticed by Ivon, who thought it odd. Strange, thought Ivon.

Phil told Ivon that the auditors were making progress and that it would take three more weeks of fieldwork. "That was a good idea," said Phil. "three years of certified financial statements adds credibility to the company. We should thank your friend Laura Standish since it was her idea."

Phil continued, "That young lady is so impressive, Ivon. She really knows her stuff and all that Wall Street mumble jumbo. She knows where she is going for sure. Listen, Ivon, sign nothing with her or her company until we get our legal people to pore over every line of all those agreements and contracts."

"Now that you mention it, I have a proposal from her firm now. Make a copy for yourself and pass it to Margaret Orr in Legal, and then let me know what you think."

About thirty minutes later, Cowboy had the large diagram unfolded and spread on the floor, large boards standing against the corner wall, and smaller slats leaning against Dr. Bates' desk. When he removed his Bates blue shirt and draped it on one of the large slats, Ivon saw Cowboy had on a sleeveless DKNY black T-shirt. Loud knocks made them turn and look toward the door. Alex Panagora trundled in and the office filled up with the loud scent of after-shave lotion.

"Is that young man your new *sho-o-ffeh*?" Casting a haughty look in Cowboy's direction, Alex leaned over, and lowering his voice, he said, "And this is the future, the *groit* white hope of

America? Look at that idi-o-tic haircut the lad sports! The impudency!"

Ivon turned to business. "Phil, please ask Joey to stop and step out. He can continue after the meeting."

"Let him be, Ivon," said Alex. "*Noinddy noin* percent of our *discashan* will go 'uveh his head; he doesn't *stroike* me as being an intellectual giant."

Pulling Alex's thick memo, Ivon set it on the low table. "I've read your memo carefully, Alex, and I thank you for some ideas that you have highlighted. But I want to address the most important issue."

"The presidency?"

"Exactly. The answer is no. I'm going to continue to be the president of the company until the finances are more settled. We have severe cash flow problems and…"

"Ivon, me boy—*yer* a green chap with no experience '*soever* in business. This *compane*e is going to go down the chutes without tough leadership because ye can't lead if you don't 'ave a *partickler* plan…"

"I have plans, and I've made my decision."

Alex snapped. "An unwise *deceeshon* that shows *yer* inexperience."

Phil, who had been quiet thus far, said: "Alex, you're being disrespectful."

Ivon stayed cool. "I recognize, Alex, that you have contributed to our growth, and that you are a master sales agent. But about two-thirds of our labor force is from minority groups and to have you as president would be irresponsible on my part."

"Are ye saying I'm biased?" Alex's voice became shrill.

Ivon shrugged. "Alex, listen to yourself. You're a racist and a bigot!"

Alex screamed. "But they are animals! Yet, out of the *koinness* of me heart, just the other die I gave *foiv* bucks to a black transsexual cross *draisser* who was begging on the street. A low life AIDS-infected faggot who should be put out of his *mis-e-ree*!"

Phil coughed into his fist, a cough that eloquently seemed to say, "See what I mean, Ivon? I told you Alex was a homophobic jerk capable of murder." Ivon caught Phil's meaning, but he only shrugged. "The president must be responsible for all his employees."

"If you *recklet* me memo *contoins* a plan," Alex argued, "*detoiling* how by down-soizing the old *toimers* the company can *soive* money."

Ivon shook his head. "All that's contrary to my beliefs and let me tell you there'll be no downsizing at Bates, let alone firing old timers! They—the old-timers like Lenox Davis, and father and Sabino—built the company, Alex. If it wasn't for them, there'd be no company!"

"Ivon, me lad, ye have no *oidea* how I've worked my *arse* off *moiking* this *compan*ee grow: the long hours, the endless *woit* in doctors offices to close sales, the *hee-u-m-ee-liashons* in getting around receptionists, secretaries, and screeners—I could go on. What about the proposal for ten percent ownership in the *compan*ee?" Sticking his chin out defiantly, Alex continued: "A very thin *sloic*e of the *poi* for the millions I've sold."

"Alex, it is your job to sell. You're the V.P. of Marketing and you are the highest paid employee. Your salary is the highest in the company. Besides, you receive commissions and you earned more than a million dollars last year."

"Almost a million and a half," jumped in Phil. "If you count the expense account, the company car, tuition for the kids, and other perks…"

"Confound the perks!" exclaimed Alex with an angry look at Phil.

From the side of his mouth, a ball of spittle descended to his chin, and as he rose to his feet, Alex whirled to hide his bloated, red face. Pacing back and forth as if in deep thought, his face broke out in a heavy sweat, which mixed with his after-shave lotion, exuded an offending odor.

Phil said, "Alex, settle down and please sit. Say what you have to say and get it over with, don't walk away with festering resentment. Let's finish this discussion."

"Shut up, Phil, and stop kissing Ivon's *arse*—you meddling scoundrel!"

"Alex, sit down," said Ivon in a firm voice. "Bates Pharmaceuticals has only two owners: Cecilia Van Osburgh and myself, and no one else. I will ask you, as politely as I know, how to leave Cecilia out of this. I understand you hounded her this past summer trying to influence her. You're not to go to her and lobby for favors—don't even go near her! Do I make myself clear? To be fair, and in view of your years of service as the company grew, I will consider an override on your commissions based on a laddered volume of sales."

"Hang the laddered soils!" Alex grabbed his thick memo and once again rose to his feet. Out of control, he slammed the memo on the low table and pointed a finger to Ivon,

"Listen, you little prick, you think you can…"

Ivon interrupted him. "This meeting is over. Get out of my office! I'll talk to you again when you are rational and more respectful."

Turning to Phil in wild panic, Alex said, "Phil, tell this lad he's going to be sorry. I *moid* this company! I brought all the big accounts, all the HMOs, all the large hospitals and *proivet* clinics. Without me there's no *Boites* Pharmaceuticals—no *companee*!"

"You heard him, get out!" said Phil as he stood up to face Alex. His thick glasses slid to the tip of his nose. Pushing back his glasses, he also pushed back his droopy shoulders, his eyes burning like red-hot coals. Ivon was surprised by Phil's stance.

Alex didn't budge.

Cowboy, who had somehow sensed Alex's early unkind remarks about him, was now holding and studying a diagram. Tossing it aside, he picked up a black slat that was leaning against Ivon's desk, and walked up to Alex with firm steps and faced him.

"You heard the Doc, get out!"

"Who asked ye, ye stupid moron!"

Cowboy jammed the slat just below Alex's diaphragm, knocking the wind out of him. Cowboy put the slat under Alex's chin.

"Get out!" Cowboy barked in Alex's face. "Move it!"

Alex jumped back and out he went.

"That's some weird, nasty dude, Doc." Without saying another word, he returned to his task.

"You see, Ivon." said Phil. "He is greedy and a plotter…no wonder Detective Wilkins thinks he killed your father. He may also be behind that note you got in your apartment…trying to scare you so that he can be president. He wants to be president at any cost."

Suddenly, Ivon's door slammed wide open and Alex walked

back in with a demented look on his face. "I'm going to sue the pants off *ye* me boy. Just wait. Ye will hear from my solicitor. I moid this *companee* and I will sue for half of it. Forget about that *miserlee* ten percent—*nawt* will satisfy me, but fifty percent!"

Ivon stood up and said: "Alex, with threats like that you leave me no choice.

"You're fired!"

Picking up the same slat, Cowboy again stepped up to Alex who quickly recoiled and yelled, "*Stoi awoi* ye damned *leeberal* radical gangster—*bastid*!" He turned and trudged off red-eyed, mumbling, "Me barrister, get me barrister…" Just then Blow Hard Myrna rushed in, enormous chest heaving as she shook a bony fist up in the air.

"Shame on you, Ivon! Alex built this company, and this is the way you reward a loyal executive. You will pay dearly for this unfair dismissal."

Feeble, melancholy rays of sunshine slanted through the window behind Phil's desk, making Cowboy's well-shaped, golden-haired forearms glisten with perspiration. Cowboy stood still.

Placing her right arm around Alex's waist, Myrna steered him around and behind a wall of gray filing cabinets. Dr. Bates watched the staff gather in clusters, talking quietly, slapping each other's backs, aghast and confused at what they had witnessed.

Cowboy swaggered back to Ivon's office.

In that instant, Ivon knew—and contrary to what Phil said—that Alex couldn't have killed his father. No way! Alex is a sorry, spineless coward. Phil and Detective Wilkins are wrong, someone else killed father. A calculating killer with ice in his or her veins is loose, perhaps ready to kill again. Oh—God. To be killed! He blinked and a hellish image rose in his mind: he saw his own body in a redbrick coffin, flaming and burning with white-hot heat, the bricks blistering and cracking and trapping him. Yes, a hellish thing is about to happen. How does one deal with the evil ways of the world? As he stepped into his office, he thought of Cassandra's words, You will lose…the laurel, the trunk, the plant, and the off-shoots: an evil seed and a good seed.

Could she possibly mean the Bates Plant? Oh, my God! Something's going to happen there. An accident? Red bricks and flames? A strong wind of foreboding, of insight, of prevision of a mean unfolding calamity gusted around him. So unfit and inadequate did he feel he wanted to run away. It is so easy to yield and withdraw into that blank barren zone of cowardice. Not having felt such a strong premonition in the past, he immediately called Sabino.

# Chapter 26 — Rendezvous at Daniela's

At 11 p.m., Wednesday night, the Orbis team left midtown Manhattan to rendezvous at Daniela's parking lot. Helen McCain drew a deep breath, thinking, "Finally, the Orbis team is on the move!" January $17^{th}$, midnight, was the zero hour for the break in. Freddy Morales and Crazy-Hose Beasley were in the lead car with Morales at the wheel. Driving the second car was Chief Lowmax, with Danny Finzicontini, the rookie, in the passenger seat, and Helen McCain in the back.

With the traffic so thick and slow on the West Side Highway, the car felt like a hearse moving at a funeral pace. Soon they blended into the George Washington Bridge traffic.

They rode in eerie silence.

McCain saw the lead car up ahead slowing down, taillights blinking. She squinted and peered into the heart of darkness to her right, into the inevitable Hudson River. All that mass of water rolling like a scaly serpent slowly crawling to its appointed fate: to be swallowed up by an even greater serpent, which is the sea. McCain thought: Human nature mimicking nature, for we are—that is Orbis Laboratories—about to swallow Bates Pharmaceuticals, like a bull shark gulps a pup porpoise.

Chief Lowmax said, "We'll be there in twenty minutes, Helen."

"I know, Lester," said McCain calmly. Her breathing turned thick, feeling her heart bursting, stinging. She said, "I know the area well because I own a house in Ridgefield Park, where I spend my weekends—not far from here."

They fell into an electric silence again.

* * * *

As they left the George Washington Bridge, the lead car with Morales and Beasley went out of sight. Lowmax rasped, "They are just up ahead."

McCain saw Danny jerk his head back against the headrest and bring his hands to his ears and squirm as if he had a severe migraine.

"Danny? Are you all right?" asked McCain.

"Yes, m'am," he stammered, as if snapping from a trance.

Lowmax didn't volunteer that Danny was on Depreprine, a drug known for its side effects: momentary rigidity and mild involuntary tremors. Chief Lowmax had been sketchy about the explosives, and since McCain wanted to know more about the "bricks" she asked Danny, "Does everyone in the SEALs learn to make bombs, Danny?"

"Everybody gets some training. But I went for advanced training at the Naval Ship Warfare Center in Maryland, where they teach you everything you need to know about underwater acoustics and detonation."

"Listen, Danny," said McCain. "May I see your machete for a minute?"

"Of course."

Danny passed the weapon to her. "I wouldn't pull it out while we're riding," he cautioned. "The slightest bump could lop off a finger, even a whole hand!" McCain held the machete with both hands, feeling its weight, and then she leaned her face against the cold scabbard. She returned the weapon to Danny. "Could you buy me one like it, Danny? Such a beautiful weapon."

"Sure. You'll have it inside a week."

McCain said, "This part of Jersey was nothing but miles and miles of wetlands."

"Look! The sign."

"We'll pass the guard shack soon, then make a left to Daniela's Restaurant—in the parking lot." Lowmax's voice sounded less nervous, but his hands were now trembling. As the moment of truth neared, Helen McCain felt energized, but not nervous, just cranked up—wired. Images of the Panopticon flashed through her mind. Let's see if Lowmax is a good field officer. Often these desk people can be long on theory but short on action. Then she saw Daniela's restaurant. At 11:35 p.m. they assembled and listened to chief Lowmax. "Get that sucker in the guardhouse, Danny, and I don't have to tell you how. I don't want any surprises from him. Just don't kill him—you follow? There'll be no killing here tonight, so that if things get messy, no one will pay much attention to a break in. The police will treat it as an accident or a bungled third-rate burglary and the whole thing dies soon."

"Aye, chief—no sweat."

"I want Freddy to be your backup. Freddy, you stay twenty yards behind Danny, just in case there's over one sucker in the guardhouse. When you have the checkpoint secured, shine your flashlight three times."

Beasley protested. "C'mon, chief, let me go with Danny. Let Freddy drive." Lowmax glared at Beasley. "I want to save you to take care of the dogs, Zach. I want to see how good you are with that baton you love so much. I don't give a rat's ass if you kill the dogs, but I don't want you to kill the guard or anyone. *Comprende*?"

Impressed by Lowmax's leadership, Helen McCain watched Danny spin on his heels and sail off into the shadows, fleet-footed and graceful, silk-smooth as if his feet weren't touching the ground. Freddy Morales trailed with camel-like hops, crunching the gravel right behind Danny. No finesse in these Puerto Ricans: rough, clumsy, tumbling. Oh well, he is loyal. In a moment, Helen McCain squinted hard to see through the glass inside the guardhouse. Suddenly, she saw two silhouettes, which in a blink disappeared, but two seconds later, the flashlight flickered three times. They drove on and picked up Danny and Freddy by the guard shack, driving straight to the parking lot, and then right to the front gates. It was 11:46 p.m.

Pleased, McCain wanted to scream with satisfaction. At 12:00 midnight they were to get inside the building, and once inside, Freddy Morales was to back up Danny, whose job was to set and detonate the bombs, while Beasley was to get rid of the dogs. Since Danny needed some space to maneuver—to set the timers in the bombs and to make a clear getaway—Captain Beasley and Sergeant Morales had to support Danny and follow his requests. This was a problem, since he was only a rookie, while Morales and Beasley were veterans, and now they had to follow orders from the rookie.

To direct operations, Chief Lowmax and Helen McCain were to remain outside as lookouts, controlling radio communication. It's such a chilly night, Helen thought. At two minutes before midnight, they returned and Chief Lowmax assembled them. "All right, men. We all know what we have to do, so let's go in and do it right. I don't want no crap, no screw-ups. Helen and I will stay here by

the cars. When you get in, wait for commo check one. Once you're on the move I'll call for commo check two. From then on, we'll break radio silence only in case of emergency." Lowmax stared at Beasley and said, "You know the layout, right Zach? I assume you have the map you and Morales got from that Loco guy."

The blackness of the night, the howling winds, the freezing temperature, the crying of the cicadas, the wailing concert of the larger animal noises escaping from the swamp and the far, flickering stars made McCain feel humble. Then a torrent of doubt about the operation washed down her spine. Getting cold feet? Nah, but there's still plenty of time to call the whole thing off. Choking a bubbling urge to burst out with wild laughter, she clenched her fists. Doubt now scraping her womb like coarse sandpaper, a feeling that reminded her of that torturous, tormenting labor, and the hideous days of black depression following her delivery. What she could never fathom—either then or now—was why the fetus in her womb had always felt like a foreign body to her. A detestable growth. In a flash he saw herself leaning over the cradle, and then Antonia's terrified eyes reading her murderous intentions; in a flash it came to her she had allowed Antonia to run off with the baby not because of concern for its safety, but because she was afraid she'd end up in jail. A gust of freezing wind snapped her out of her reverie. It's too late to do anything about it.

Or—is it?

What the hell, what's life but a race to victory? To hear the cheers of crowning glory and success! Can't chicken out now. Narrow, dangerous is the path to glory, while wide, safe and cozy is the trail to hell—to mediocrity. No, no, the secret to a glorious life lies with those that act! Indeed, to fight for what one wants is living the right life, while to suffer wrong is the sin of the meek and the useless. Power and ambition are the parents of decisive action. Blowing warm breath onto her cold, aching palms, she snapped, "Let's go, Lowmax! The hell with your waiting around with your fingers up your rectums. Move it!" Heh, heh, heh, you have to kick a little ass sometimes.

Within a few seconds, Danny picked the lock, and they went inside. They stood about 5 yards from the stairs, orienting themselves. Morales's wireless handset crackled and Chief Lowmax's voice came in with perfect clarity. "Commo check one, commo check—you copy? Over."

"Loud and clear. Out," replied Morales.

Morales and Lowmax had gallium arsenide-based handsets—as opposed to the old silicon technology—that amplified their voices almost to perfection.

Zach Beasley signaled them to step away from the night-light. "These stairs lead to the third floor, to the research labs. Put the first brick up there, Danny. We come back here, then we go to Storage for the second brick," said Beasley, pointing to his left. "The third brick goes in the basement, by the boiler, the generator, and all the master switches."

Morales said, "Dion Loco Bromius sure drew a good map."

"I smell dog," said Danny. "I feel them dogs nearby."

Beasley snapped, "Shut up, Danny! You worry about them detonators and timers. I'll handle the stupid dogs—that's my job!"

They skulked to the stairs, Morales trailing. Unexpectedly, the doors to the right of the stairs slammed out as if someone had kicked them open.

They turned and froze on the spot.

Two dogs lunged out, viciously barking, tearing up towards the group. The dog attack was so sudden that they had no time to react. "Debates" leaped, aiming for Beasley's shiny head, but Beasley side-swept the dog with his forearm. "Rebates" went for Morales' thigh and sank his teeth in tearing up flesh and muscle, making him scream in agonizing pain, his inhuman howls resonating and filling the lonely empty halls, bays, and naves.

Bats and vampires screeched in sudden panic up in the high nave.

Beasley kicked the unyielding dog. Danny—in army tiger fatigues and blackened face—stepped up to the landing with his back against the wall, sinking deep into the shadows. He saw "Debates" skid around and recover, ears pinned back, menacing, glittering eyes and bared fangs fixing to aim for Beasley's shiny head again. Danny yelled, "Watch out Zach!"

"Debates" charged and vaulted as if urged by a conscious fury. Turning, Beasley seized the dog in mid-air, his right hand clamped around the dog's snout and twisting it. Debates' body whipped in a wide arc, crashing against the floor. Beasley drew his Colt .45, shooting Debates in the back. Baton in hand, he rained vicious, merciless blows on the dead dog.

Screaming at the top of his lungs, Morales got Beasley away from the dead dog. "Kill him!" begged Morales. But wanting to use his rubber hose, Beasley hit the obstinate dog again and again. But the dog only growled and locked his jaws deeper, as if urged by a primal instinct to shred and sever flesh from bone.

"Shoot him, Zach," shrieked Morales. "Shoot him!"

Beasley was about to shoot the dog when he saw a human shape draw out of the shadows and lunge at him, attempting to wrestle the gun away from him. Beasley re-angled the gun—with stunning speed for a big man—and took a shot at the heart area of the lunging shape, and he watched the shape collapse in a heap at his feet.

"I'll be damned—it's an old man!" said Danny.

Beasley pointed the gun, aiming to take another shot at the old man, but Morales' ungodly screams got his attention. Instead, he rained a hail of blows on the dog with his baton, but the dog didn't let go. Finally, Beasley put the gun on the dog's ear and pulled the trigger.

Beasley grabbed the handset, "Sierra-3, Sierra-3—you copy?" "What's the problem? Over," replies Lowmax.

"We had a delay with the dogs and the watchman, an old man. I took care of them. Morales eighty-sixed. Request instructions. Are we still on with the initial plan?"

"Negative. Second Isaiah. Negative! You only have time for two bricks. Proceed to Storage and then the boiler and the POL. Disregard the third floor—repeat: do not go to the lab on the third floor. Read me back. Over."

"Only two bricks: Storage and boiler, generator, plus petroleum, oil, and other lubricants. Forget about the third floor. Wilco—out."

Beasley eyed Morales' wounds. "Deep flesh wound, Freddy. You stay put." He pulled Morales' belt out and fixed a tourniquet. "Danny and I will pick you up in five to seven minutes—don't you panic. We'll be back shortly. Just hang on, buddy."

"You come back and get me, Zach," pleaded Morales in a weak voice, eyes glittering with terror. "Don't leave me here, Zach—we've been friends for a long time."

"Don't you worry none, buddy. You got my word." Beasley and Danny took off to set off the bombs. And as promised, they returned within seven minutes.

"Let's get the hell out of here," said Danny. "Them timers are set for five more minutes."

"What happened to the old man?" asked Danny. "I thought he was dead—hey, Morales, where in the hell is the old man?"

Morales groaned, "I saw him crawl thatta way. He checked the dogs and then he burst out cursing, like them dogs were babies or human beings. Never seen anybody care so much for dead dogs."

"Crazy old fool! He took a bullet for a dog," said Danny.

"He'll die soon enough, that bullet hit him dead center in the chest," said Beasley. "He couldn't have gotten that far…but we can't waste time looking for the body, we have less than three minutes to get out of here."

Putting Morales between them, they carried him out.

# Chapter 27 — Sabino's Valiant Defense

"Hurry!" urged McCain. And just as they skidded around the guard shack, the bombs went off, bright red orange flames lighting up the sky. Although the traffic on the highway was sparse, Chief Lowmax drove with caution. At the first stop light he slowed down, coming to a full stop, which made McCain lose her patience yelling, "Go through the lights, Lester, Crissakes! Or we'll be sitting here waiting to be caught by the highway patrol."

Running through the stoplights, hands clenching the steering wheel, Lowmax speeded up. "You see Zach, Danny?" He asked with a tremulous voice.

"Yeah, chief. They are right behind us. Morales must be in pain; that goddamned dog almost tore his leg off."

"Is Zach hurt?" asked Lowmax.

"He's all right," said Danny. "He shot them dogs and beat the hell out of them with his rubber hose; he hit one of them right in the snout a million times. He was going to shoot the dog that had latched on to Freddy's leg when the old man jumped in front of the dog and took the bullet in the chest."

Helen McCain groused, "What old man, Lester? You said only two dogs guarded the Plant, and that there was no night watchman inside."

"The old man came out of nowhere, like a ghost. I kid you not. I swear I almost peed my pants," said Danny. "A crazy old man to die for a stupid dog."

"This highway has too many stop lights! I'll be glad when we get to the George Washington Bridge," whined Lowmax.

Danny exclaimed, "Hey, chief. Something is wrong! Slow down. Look at their headlights; they are going crazy all over the highway. Something is totally wrong, man. Another car is behind them, bumping them, running them out of the highway."

Slowing down and then coming to a full stop on the shoulder of the highway, Lowmax turned around just in time to see Zach Beasley's car fly off into the trees. They waited for a few seconds in dead silence; then they saw a lone silhouette loping along in the dim glow of the amber lights.

"I don't believe this!" said Danny. "It's the old man; I recognize that white hair. I'll be damned—he's alive! We left him for dead and I was sure he was dead; nobody can survive a bullet at point blank from a Colt.45. Man, that.45 ball is heavy…impossible…"

Helen McCain cursed, "Lester, goddamn it, you did a half-ass job. Now we have trouble. That's no ordinary old man, that's Sabino Yamamoto! I warned you repeatedly to keep tabs. He's the only man I've ever feared in my life, and he's coming after us now!"

"He's got a shotgun," said Danny.

McCain marveled at Danny's night vision. Danny can see what others can't. "What do we do, chief? Shall I see?" asked Danny, eager to prove himself before McCain.

"Stay put, Danny. They're big boys; they can take care of their own damned selves." Lowmax looked at Helen McCain as if asking, "What do we do now?"

McCain grumbled, "Let's wait a while." She waited, not because she was unconcerned about Beasley and Morales, but because she knew that the wily old man would lurk in the vicinity lying in wait. Before long, they watched Sabino advance, holding the shotgun like a toy, slowly marching toward the gloom. Beasley's car had flown off a ravine, crashing against the trunk of a large oak tree.

Sabino surveyed the area. Shining in an upward incongruous tilt, the right head beam was still on, the driver's front side a mess of twisted metal and shattered glass, glass shards glittering like mica under the tall lamppost from which a halogen lamp cast pallid amber light.

"You!" Sabino shouts to the driver. "Come out of the car before I blow your head off."

Beasley was semi-conscious, groggy, his shiny baldhead lolling.

Noticing that the other man slumped against the dashboard, Sabino yanked the driver's door open, placing the shotgun against Beasley's left temple; a thin stream of blood was flowing from Beasley's left ear. He grabbed the man's collar behind his thick neck and dragged him out of the car. When Sabino opened the man's jacket to pull the gun from the holster, he felt a long baton under the strap of the holster. What's this? It's a damn billy club, a rubber hose. Tossing Beasley's gun into the bushes, he kept the truncheon. So, this is the stick this gorilla killed Rebates and Debates with. Stepping around the wreckage, Sabino tried to drag the other man out of the car, but he was too heavy; he looked at the man's leg and he saw the gore. Just then, Morales opened his eyes only to see the old man's harsh stare, his droopy eyelid twitching. A dull light seeped out of Morales' terror-engorged eyes as Sabino's 10-inch blade sliced the Puerto Rican's liver sideways. Then Sabino heard Beasley moan.

The big ape is coming around.

Sitting up—his eyes unfocused, cross-eyed, wheezing and taking big gulps of air—Beasley then groped for the side of the car, scooting against it. Sabino watched him struggle to regain consciousness, which he did in a few seconds, his eyes widening as he recognized the old man towering over him.

"I thought you were dead, old man," rasped Beasley, with no remorse in his scratchy voice. "What are you doing with my rubber hose?" Beasley reached for his gun, but his arm hanged disobediently lifeless to the side.

Smacking the arm with the rubber hose, Sabino then whacked Beasley's face back and forth, rocking his cone-head sideways with each blow. A blow to the septum crackled like the flap of a bat's wings, as red-black blood drained out from both nostrils flooding Beasley's mouth; a mouth wide open and gasping for air.

"You like the taste of blood, uh?"

"Give me my rubber hose—*eemeemagoovehoz,*" Beasley slurred. "Then you can shoot me, old timer." Sabino saw him clench his right fist. He could read the man's eyes that seemed to say, "In two more minutes, I'll rip your balls off, old timer."

Putting the shotgun down, Sabino drew his Sevillana blade and just as the hulking mass of Beasley's arm lunged for his throat, the old man sunk the 10-inch blade deep into the hulking man's barrel chest, just below his diaphragm. Beasley's eyes bulged to twice their size, the bloodshot pupils resembling deviled eggs sprinkled with paprika.

"You can't die yet, you big ape."

When Sabino drew the blade straight out, Beasley's head jerked backward, banging loudly against the car door. "Shoot me," Beasley rasped, "with the shotgun, old man."

"Oh, no. You hit my dogs in the mouth and made pulp out of

them and killed them. It's only fair that you die by your mouth, too." Using his blade, he pried Beasley's jaws open and shoved the rubber hose down the dying man's throat and airway until he couldn't push it down anymore. Beasley sucked air through nose, mouth, and hose, finally letting out a bloodcurdling honk. Only after he ascertained that the big ape was dead, did Sabino sling the shotgun on his good shoulder to walk back to the highway, the same highway that during daylight hours bustled with strident, piling, vibrant traffic, was now silent, desolate, and lifeless.

* * * *

Squirming in their seats and peering hard into the darkness, McCain, Lowmax, and Danny saw the old man return to his pickup, make a U-turn, and drive south. As they watched the tailgate lights fade into the night, Helen McCain ordered Lowmax, "Go see what happened and come right back. We shouldn't hang around here for too long. Danny, leave your gun with me, and make sure it's loaded with the safety latch off."

Like two desperate ghosts, Lowmax and Danny melded into the darkness, reaching the scene of the wreck within a minute. When Danny lifted Beasley's head up to get a better look, he nearly froze with horror at the gruesome sight. He saw the tip-end of the hose sticking out of Beasley's mouth, eyeballs rolled up, staring as if he was still alive. After a few seconds of disbelief, Danny said, "How in the hell can anyone abuse a corpse in such a brutal fashion? This is a sickening sight."

"Did Beasley swallow his tongue?" Lowmax asked, peering over Danny's shoulder.

"No, chief. The old man rammed the hose down his gullet!"

"I'll be damned and go to hell if that Sabino isn't a damned psycho, to do that to a dying man. This is the piss poor act of a cruel, mean fiend. Is Morales dead too?"

"Think so, chief."

"Let's help Freddy. Man, some awful way to die; but then again, old Crazy-Hose Beasley loved that damn hose more than he loved his own dick. He took it with him, all right."

Pulling Beasley out of the way and climbing inside the cab,

Danny examined Morales. "Freddy's dead, too! He bled to death, chief. His leg is a bloody mess; it's all torn to shreds and his gut is cut sideways."

"Are you sure he's dead? Maybe he's just passed out."

"Yeah, chief," yelled Danny. "His clothes are all ripped and smeared with blood. Looks like he bathed in blood, a bloody mess!" He drew out of the car. "What should…"

Terrified, unable to finish his question, Danny seemed paralyzed, as if he was seeing the devil himself standing a few yards behind the chief's back. Lowmax turned around to see what Danny was so intently gazing at. What's he looking at? Must be a damned rigidity attack from his medication! A few steps up the ravine, Lowmax saw the old man's eyes shining like glowing embers, his face a deadly pallor. Lowmax's eyes flashed with animal panic. Must hit the dirt! But fear had paralyzed him.

Overcoming his bout of rigidity and reaching for his dagger, Danny aimed at the old timer's heart, letting it fly. But a tremor froze his arm in midair, making him waste a precious second, causing the blade to sink into the old man's shoulder instead.

In the next second, Danny and Lowmax saw the shotgun thrust a tongue of flames that came rushing and engulfing them and hurling them against the side of the car. Lowmax's immense body took the shot, shielding Danny, who flew through the air rolling into the dark thicket. Sabino heard the rustle of the fleeing man scampering at full speed into the dark woods. Next, he blasted the gas tank and the car and the three bodies blew up streaking the night with brilliant orange flames.

Pulling the dagger out with a quick jerk, Sabino looked at the fake jewels that adorned the handle and disdainfully tossed it into the burning bush. As he hobbled on the highway, Sabino snorted as if he was trying to expel the stench of burned flesh and human hair that had stuck in his nostrils. Touching the wound on his chest, he bent down for a few seconds, straightening up with painful jerks, and then headed south to his pickup. The stars were out, far, fixed, studding the sky with crowded twinkling points. The night is immense; he thought. And yet he felt trapped in an eerie timeless space, much like a yolk in an eggshell—enclosed in deadened loneliness; trapped in a time that feels both barren and non-human, with no rhythm, no day, and no night."

* * * *

Having escaped the shotgun blast with only minor scrapes, Danny returned to Helen McCain, and in a nervous chatter, he told her that Beasley, Morales, and Lowmax were all dead. "I can't get this picture of Captain Beasley out of my mind."

"What picture?"

"The way he died. When I first saw him, I thought I was looking at an anteater. You know that silly hose he carried with him? Well, that thing was sticking out of his mouth, and in a way, it was kind of comical. Looked like he was sticking his tongue out at me."

Within seconds, they both saw Sabino's solitary silhouette zigzag down the highway and fade into the gloomy night.

"All right, Danny. Drive north slowly," said Helen McCain.

"Ain't no traffic, ma'am," responded Danny. "I can open up and be out of here in no time."

"No, Danny. Just drive slowly, I know why." McCain was smiling, but instead she wanted to laugh, to stamp her feet, and scream. These security people are a joke, and where do they get off calling themselves security when they're so unreliable. Expect neither a fine job nor a quality show from low-quality people. Unable to hold her silent ruminations, she blabbered, "Oh, Sabino, you goddamn monster! You're a man with brass balls. This is the second chief of security Orbis has lost to you. You crafty kidnapper, you snatched Rashkin to avenge Joe Bates' death, but Rashkin didn't kill Joe. I did! I did! Heh heh heh, don't rob me of my glory. Yes, the deed was mine."

To Danny: "The old man will be along in a few minutes. Just give him a chance to catch up. Wounded and bleeding to death like a lone wolf, he can't go for too long with a bullet in his chest. And since you guys left him for dead, he must be in terrible shape." Utter silence seemed to have cascaded into the night; nowhere was there sign of life until, out of the darkness, two high beams erupted into the night. Grabbing Danny's Walther semi-automatic, she cried, "Steady, Danny—Sabino's coming after us. Around this area people call Sabino Mister muchos cojones! You see him in the mirror now?"

"Yeah, I see the pickup, ma'am."

"Helen, Danny—call me Helen. You're a survivor. I will give you a bonus of five thousand dollars for doing well tonight. You earned it."

"Thanks, m-m—Helen," said Danny. "He's getting closer."

Although they had braced themselves, Sabino's head-on ram jolted them. Next, the rear window exploded, deafening them, causing Danny to swerve all over the highway, thinly missing a station wagon speeding south in the other lane. Danny held on. With the Walther in hand, McCain took a few shots, as if getting the feel for the gun, and then steadying the gun with two hands. She blasted away.

Zigzagging and side-sweeping, Sabino dodged the blast, and closing in, he crashed into the right rear fender. Danny cursed, the car skidding against the metal guardrail, sparks flying and lighting up the night. Then they saw Sabino's pickup come to a full stop. Danny stopped, too. Pressing the trigger, and with the bursts sounding more like a high-powered jackhammer breaking steel than gun reports, McCain almost emptied the whole clip. Then, taking deep breaths, and so pumping badly needed oxygen into both her lungs and heart, she felt high, young and invigorated. Oh, how she loved the thrill of the night.

"I've got another clip here," said Danny. "I'll load it for you."
"Wait, Danny."

They waited for one minute—risking arrest by the Highway Patrol—to see, much to their relief, the pickup make a U-turn and head south. Helen McCain smiled. "I must have hit the crusty old geezer."

"That old man killed three good men, Helen—all by himself. Three tough, good, and experienced men and he would have killed me too if I hadn't moved fast."

"Three men, I agree. But if they were any tough and good, they'd be alive!" "I guess that makes us tough and good—right?"

"All right, Danny, drive on."

To Helen, the cold air felt just fine; it had been so long since she'd felt such a wild state of exhilaration that she took a moment to calm down. Feeling giddy and afraid that she might swoon, she quickly gave Danny directions to her place in New Jersey, where they would spend the night.

Danny tore off with a loud squeal of tires, reaching Broad Avenue, where he turned west on U. S. 46 toward Ridgefield Park.

"We'll stay at my place in Ridgefield Park tonight. This is my secret hideaway, my sanctuary, so you must promise to be discrete. You can't reveal this to anyone, okay, Danny?"

"You got it. I am a Brooklyn guy, never been to Jersey in my whole life." Never had Helen McCain felt so young, energized her, shoulders resting square against the seat. Finally, unable to restrain herself, she burst out with a loud cackling, hysterical laughter. "The only person who knows about my house is Antonia," she said out loud. "But I doubt if she remembers where it is, since I only brought her here once or twice to clean it up."

Peering into the rear-view mirror, Danny tried to see her face, but it was too dark. He squirmed and pushed the gas pedal, with his eyes glittering, as if he was having a dialogue with himself. "Is she out of her mind?" "Oh, no—she's just wired." "What a tough, crazy woman! She did mumble that she had killed someone; that the deed was done. What deed was she talking about? And who's Antonia?"

"You know how to operate that Control Room, Danny?"

"Aye, Chief Lowmax taught me a few things, but I've been learning on my own, too, and by now I know the major functions."

"Excellent. I'm going to put you in charge there."

"I'm only a rookie…some of the guys will get jealous."

"Don't you worry about that," McCain reassured him. "I will hire a new chief and we will rebuild the force, but you will report to me directly. Besides, I think I will need a bodyguard as things heat up. You're special. You are a survivor like me, so stick with me and you'll see that together we're going to win. We lost three men tonight, and we'll remember that they sacrificed their lives for the good of our cause. But we crippled Bates Pharmaceuticals, and there's no way they can ship anything out for a long time."

"That was a beautiful explosion," said Danny. "I have no words to paint the colors of the flames: orange, purples, pinks. It seemed the colors talked to each other in flaming tongues! Oh, Helen—thanks for bringing me here tonight!"

Almost suffocating, her lips twitching with unbearable excitement, she exclaimed, "They're hurting now. No sales, no cash, no sales, no cash, no sales — no shit!"

"They're in deep shit," echoed Danny.

"Listen, Danny. It won't be too long before they collapse, because we've got them by the balls. If anyone comes around asking you questions, just say you were never here in New Jersey, okay? Yoh, what'd a Brooklyn dude be doing in Jersey? —*Joisie.* You just hang tough. Deny. Deny. But be a little smart, too, and throw them a bone, 'Maybe them guys overspent for Christmas and needed cash and thought up a quick hit.'

"Got it. Guy overspend for the holidays and are left with a pile of unpaid bills. So, instead of cursing—*coising*— their spending habits, they look for easy cash."

"Yeah, something like that: 'guys were acting independently, not unusual for security people to double dip here and there.' No one will have the balls to question me! Nobody questions the Uberfrau!"

END OF PART I

CPSIA information can be obtained
at www.ICGtesting.com
Printed in the USA
BVHW070836130223
658300BV00014B/422